## Bolan ... ugh the door connecting the train cars.

Crouching, they made for the door at the far end of the car. Bolan flung it open and hustled Sherman through. They paused on the swaying, open platform between the two cars, the rattle and rumble of the train loud in their ears.

The ground swept by, a spread of green below the slope that bordered the track.

Bolan glanced back and saw armed figures moving into view. This time he held the Beretta in both hands and fired. Glass shattered. Bolan saw one man fall, and the others pulled aside. The delay would only last for seconds. He holstered the 93R and zipped up his jacket.

"You ever jump from a moving train?"

Sherman stared at Bolan. "Hell, no," he said.

"First time for everything."

# MACK BOLAN ®
## The Executioner

# THE EXECUTIONER®

### DON PENDLETON'S

## KILL SQUAD

## A GOLD EAGLE BOOK FROM

# WORLDWIDE®

TORONTO • NEW YORK • LONDON
AMSTERDAM • PARIS • SYDNEY • HAMBURG
STOCKHOLM • ATHENS • TOKYO • MILAN
MADRID • WARSAW • BUDAPEST • AUCKLAND

First edition March 2016

ISBN-13: 978-0-373-64446-9

Special thanks and acknowledgment to
Mike Linaker for his contribution to this work.

Kill Squad

Recycling programs
for this product may
not exist in your area.

**Printed in U.S.A.**

Honorable actions are ascribed by us to virtue, and dishonorable actions to vice; and only a madman would conclude that these judgments are matters of opinion, and not fixed by nature.

—Marcus Tulius Cicero,
106–43 BC

There is no honor in the Mob, human vultures who prey upon the weak and the innocent, their sole purpose to make money. But there are good people who fight the good fight, and we will stand with them until our last breath.

—Mack Bolan

# THE
# MACK BOLAN
## LEGEND

Nothing less than a war could have fashioned the destiny of the man called Mack Bolan. Bolan earned the Executioner title in the jungle hell of Vietnam.

But this soldier also wore another name—Sergeant Mercy. He was so tagged because of the compassion he showed to wounded comrades-in-arms and Vietnamese civilians.

Mack Bolan's second tour of duty ended prematurely when he was given emergency leave to return home and bury his family, victims of the Mob. Then he declared a one-man war against the Mafia.

He confronted the Families head-on from coast to coast, and soon a hope of victory began to appear. But Bolan had broken society's every rule. That same society started gunning for this elusive warrior—to no avail.

So Bolan was offered amnesty to work within the system against terrorism. This time, as an employee of Uncle Sam, Bolan became Colonel John Phoenix. With a command center at Stony Man Farm in Virginia, he and his new allies—Able Team and Phoenix Force—waged relentless war on a new adversary: the KGB.

But when his one true love, April Rose, died at the hands of the Soviet terror machine, Bolan severed all ties with Establishment authority.

Now, after a lengthy lone-wolf struggle and much soul-searching, the Executioner has agreed to enter an "arm's-length" alliance with his government once more, reserving the right to pursue personal missions in his Everlasting War.

# Prologue

*Las Vegas, Nevada*

Harry Sherman knew there was a problem the moment he stepped inside Marco Conte's spacious office. The casino boss sat behind his massive desk, his narrowed gaze drilling into him.

His bodyguard, Milo Forte, was seated beside him. Forte was a big man, well muscled beneath his well-cut suit, and Sherman knew he had a fearsome reputation. He was ready to act the moment his boss snapped his fingers. A pair of Conte's hardmen stood near the desk, flanking Sol Lemke. They kept the man upright because he was unable to stand on his own.

Lemke was one of the accountants who worked under Sherman in the accounting department. It took him a few moments to recognize his subordinate, who had been beaten until his face was a swollen mess. There was excessive blood. His nose was flattened and his pulped mouth hung open, dribbling blood from his lacerated lips and gums down his shirtfront. From the way his left arm hung, it was obvious that it was broken and his left hand was a misshapen, finger-crushed mess.

Marco Conte ran the Vegas casino with a firm hand. He intimidated those who worked under him while presenting a genial face to the customers. No one crossed Conte. He was tough and uncompromising. From the tension in the office and the harsh expression on Conte's face, Sherman knew that something heavy was going down.

As Sherman moved into the room he heard the solid door click shut behind him. He experienced a frisson of anxiety. He had no idea what this summons was all about.

"Nine million dollars, Harry," Conte said in his low, gruff voice. "Nine. That's a shitload of money."

As the head of the casino's accounting department, Sherman knew what nine million dollars represented, but he had no idea how it related to him. Even so he was beginning to get nervous. His mouth went dry.

"Mr. Conte?"

The casino boss leaned forward.

"That's odd, Harry," he said.

"What?"

"You called me *Mr. Conte*. Not Marco. We've never used anything but first names, Harry. You sound nervous. Is there a reason why you should be nervous?"

"Mr.—Marco…can someone tell me what this is all about? Because I have no idea."

Sherman knew his voice had cracked. It came out like a croak.

"Why did I expect him to say that?" Conte asked no

one in particular. "Maybe it's because he does know what this is all about. Is that right, Sol?"

Lemke refused to meet Sherman's gaze. He pawed at his bleeding mouth with his right hand, wincing when he touched torn flesh.

"Yeah, he knows."

His voice was weak, quavering.

Sherman could feel all eyes on him. He was being accused of something, and he didn't know what.

"Gone, Harry," Conte said finally. "All that money gone. Lost."

"Or stolen," Forte added.

"He has a point, Harry. Money doesn't get up and walk away on its own."

"Marco, none of this makes sense. Where was this money?"

"The backup account," Conte said. "You remember the backup account? You should, Harry, because you look after it."

Sherman remained silent. There was a nagging voice in his head telling him he hadn't looked at the account in some time. Mainly because there was no need. The backup fund was seldom touched. Because the casino was making so much money, there was no need to dip into the reserve.

Forte raised a hamlike fist and jabbed a thick finger in Lemke's direction.

"Quit screwing 'round, Sherman. We *know*. Lemke and you took the money. He already told us."

The words stung. Sherman stared at Lemke. The man held his gaze despite the pain he was in.

"Harry," Conte said, "there's no use trying to stall.

Sol told us you were in it together. Took the nine million and shifted it to other accounts you set up."

The words hit like solid punches. Sherman was unable to speak. His mind was wrestling with the situation, trying to make sense of it all. If money was missing, he had been set up by Lemke to draw attention from himself and implicate Sherman.

"Marco, this is crazy. You really believe what he's saying? That I'd be any part of this? Come on, Marco, it's too much of a setup to be true."

"Is it?"

"Why would I even try to screw you over? What the hell would I want with nine million dollars? Don't I get paid enough to look after your books? Jesus, Marco, I'm no big spender. I don't even gamble. You're always joking about that. The only guy in Vegas who doesn't even play the slot machines. What do you think? That I've run up such a big tab I have to steal from the man I work for? Marco, just look at me. I have not done this. I would not do this to you. *Ever.*"

Conte was studying Sherman closely, searching his face for any hint of deception.

"I always trusted you, Harry. Right now I'm not so sure I should have."

"Marco, what can I say? This is down to my word against Sol's. While we're playing his game, his real partners are moving the money out of reach."

It had become very quiet. No one spoke. They were all waiting for Conte.

His decision would be final. There would be no challenge to it. If Conte made a decision, it was written in concrete. No going back. Right or wrong, his word was law.

"Okay, this is how we'll do it. Harry, you have four days to locate the missing money. I give you my word that nothing will happen to you during that time. If you don't replace the nine million, that's it. If the money isn't back where it belongs, the hammer comes down. Don't fail me, Harry. Until today I never had reason to doubt you. Don't make a fool out of me. If you're on the level, make me see that. Lemke here figured he was smart enough to put some of the take in his own account so he could skip town and collect the big prize later. He didn't know there's a check we can make on the unexpected movement of casino money. Not even you were told about it, Harry. We'll be checking your account, as well."

"Are we going to find some big deposits there?" Forte asked.

"If he's involved, I don't think Harry would be stupid enough to do something like that," Conte said. "It's your move, Harry. Make my money come back. Four days."

One of Conte's men opened the door. As Sherman stepped through and the door began to close behind him, he heard Conte speaking again.

"Not you, Lemke. We have a lot more to discuss…"

Sherman made his way to his office, ignoring the other members of the department. He stepped inside, closed the door, sat at his desk and was suddenly overcome with a feeling of utter loneliness. In a building full of people he was totally on his own, with the clock already starting its slide to zero.

The only thing Sherman knew for certain was that he had not taken Conte's money. Sol Lemke had fingered him to pull the heat off himself; a seemingly smart move that backfired on the man.

Conte was suspicious, even though he had cut Sherman a break. He was giving him the opportunity to return—or try to return—the missing cash. Sherman knew that even if he succeeded in retrieving the money it was not going to erase what had happened. He was under no illusions as to his eventual fate.

In the end Conte would be considering only one thing: the money. That was the single most important factor in Marco Conte's life. He didn't give a damn about anything else.

Once the deadline was reached, successful or not, Harry Sherman would become a target. He was sure the ink was already drying on his death sentence. Conte was not going to risk leaving Sherman alive. That the theft had happened was already a black mark against the man. Conte was going to do all he could to let the east coast mob know that he did not allow such transgressions to go unpunished. Sherman visualized the terrible sight of Sol Lemke—bloody and broken, with more of the same to come.

Sherman would be next. He would be another example of how Marco Conte dealt with anyone who stole from him—because stealing from him meant stealing from the organization, and that was not to be tolerated.

Harry Sherman was walking a tightrope suspended over a drop into Hell.

FORTE LEANED OVER to hear Conte's whispered words. The casino boss had made up his mind about Sol Lemke.

"Take him out of town," Conte said. "Have a couple of the boys work on him until he gives. I don't give a shit what they do. That turkey knows what this is all about. That's why he was packed and ready to skip town when the boys picked him up. I want to know who he's working with."

Forte nodded. He stood and moved toward one of the hardmen. Lemke picked up on what was being said and jerked upright, staring at Conte.

"I told you how it is, Mr. Conte. It's Sherman who's fucking with your money. Not me. That mother has jacked your money. I had nothing to do with it."

His ranting increased and the accusations poured from his bloody mouth, adding other names to his litany of blame. The shrillness rose as he pleaded for his life.

Conte eventually tired of hearing it. He made a sharp, cutting motion with his hand. Behind Lemke a pistol rose and fell, the solid blow rendering him unconscious.

"Get that piece of trash out of my office," Conte said. "The back way. Stuff him in the trunk and drive into the desert. You know where. If I didn't need him able to speak, I'd say cut out his tongue to shut him up. Hell, once he spills what he knows, you can cut it out. Make him eat it before you make him dig his own grave and bury him in it."

Lemke was dragged from the office through a back door that led directly to the basement garage.

After he had dismissed everyone except Forte, Conte asked for a drink. He sat toying with the thick tumbler.

"Do you believe Harry?" Conte asked.

Forte shrugged. "I can't decide. He's always been a straight kind of guy. Boring. But I never would have had him down as a thief. Hell, Marco, how do we know? Working with all that money every day. Moving it around. It would be a hell of a temptation. Even a guy like Harry Sherman could be tempted."

"I always liked Harry," Conte said. "He kept the accounts straight. Never caused any problems." He swallowed the contents of the tumbler and held it out for a refill. "Lemke made a good case against him. But the way Harry reacted… Jesus, Milo… I can't pin it down one way or the other. And Lemke started to lose it. He was ready to drag in any name he could think of at the end."

"If Harry's in on it, he has the chance to make it right," Forte said. "He must know you don't mess around. You gave him four days. If it's not done by then, he knows he's a dead man. I mean, what's he going to do? Run and hide?"

That made Conte think. What *would* Sherman do?

If he was in with Lemke, all he had to do was to keep playing the game until the nine million had been hidden away where it couldn't be found. Then make a run for it.

If Sherman had been set up by Lemke, he would do his best to get the money back before the deadline. If he succeeded, or failed, he would have realized he was on the edge. He could easily fake the figures to get Conte to back off and then make a run for it.

However the dice rolled, one thing was certain. Marco Conte was going to get a hard time from Serge Bulova. The east coast head honcho would be determined to put the hammer down hard—and Conte, the man on the spot in Vegas, would be the choice to catch the flak. Bulova would see this as Conte having taken his eye off the ball. The Russian wouldn't give a damn how it turned out. Money back or not, Bulova would make his displeasure known.

"Okay, put someone on Harry," Conte said. "I need to know his moves. If he steps out of line, he's finished. And when Harry's four days are up, I want him dead if he comes through or not. I have to show we don't let ourselves be played for suckers. We clean up. Make certain we're covered. Right now I got to call back east and tell Bulova we have a problem."

"He isn't going to like it."

Conte managed a mirthless smile. "You think I do, Milo? There's no easy way around this. Sooner I call Serge the better. Yeah, he isn't going to like what I have to tell him. He'll want to send that prick Danichev to stand watch over us while we sort out this mess. You know, Milo, I hate that smart-ass son of a bitch."

Conte reached for his phone and hit the speed dial number.

DESPERATE TO FIND the missing money, Sherman sat at his computer, checking the numbers for the tenth time. He was getting nowhere. As a last hope, he decided to key in a sequence of numbers he had almost forgotten about. Perhaps the money trail could somehow be picked up there.

The commands called up a series of files he had found by accident some months ago. The secret files had come into his possession during a financial data exchange between Sherman and Conte. In his haste, and most likely due to his poor computer skills, the casino boss had unknowingly sent the chief accountant a number of odd files. Sherman had never seen the lines of code before and, more out of curiosity than anything else, had saved them in a folder then deleted Conte's error.

Immediately following the incident, Sherman had felt a sense of guilt at what he had done. Even so, he'd kept the new files and continued the transfer of accounts to Conte.

Now he opened the saved files and read them one by one. Once his eyes had scanned the first few pages of the lists on his monitor, he was unable to stop. Seeing and recognizing the names, and the payoffs made to those individuals, there was no going back. No erasing the information he had seen. The names and payoffs were in his mind and there was no delete button he could press to wipe them away.

He realized that he was looking at explosive information capable of bringing down powerful people. If this information was made public, a number of influential people were going to fall hard, as would Sherman's employer and the head of Conte's organization back east. Sherman had seen the information now. It had the potential to destroy lives, and he would be in the middle of it all.

He decided to save the information on a flash drive. It was all he had; the only insurance policy that might stay Conte's hand. He only had to figure out what to do with it.

Leo Turrin leaned back in his chair, pondering his next move. Once a deep undercover agent for the Justice Department, Turrin had penetrated the closed ranks of the Mafia and become a trusted confederate. Now he was "semiretired" from the mob and worked in Justice's headquarters in Washington, DC. His current focus was a crime boss named Marco Conte.

A case board covered one wall of the little Fed's office. The current layout was a montage of information on the Conte organization. Pinned in place were numerous photos of the main players—Conte in a variety of poses, his coterie of lieutenants, lesser men in the group and photos of other criminal figures; some friends, some enemies—as well as images of buildings that included houses and office complexes, and vehicles. The board contained anything and everything relating to Marco Conte's operation.

Turrin spent a lot of time studying the information, going over what he knew and adding new data whenever it showed up.

He knew that if he got Conte, Justice would have a shot at taking down the head of the organization, Serge Bulova, an east coast crime lord.

All he wanted was the one small sliver of data that might give him his way in.

Finally his patience and dogged persistence had paid off. He'd learned from an inside source that Harry Sherman, Conte's chief accountant, was in trouble with his boss. Money was missing.

After researching Sherman, Turrin asked his source to ferret out what he could about the missing money. He had no idea if Sherman would play ball but figured he had nothing to lose and a hell of a lot to gain if Sherman turned out to be the chink in the mob's armor.

He decided to reach out to the man.

*Las Vegas, Nevada*

INTEL HAD REVEALED that Harry Sherman stopped at the same café every morning on the way to the casino.

The little Fed sat at the table behind him, watching and waiting for his moment. As Sherman briefly glanced away from the table, Turrin rose and, slipping a folded note beside the man's coffee mug, walked away. He didn't look back.

He had to wait until Sherman contacted him. If he didn't, then the Justice man would try another approach.

The next morning Turrin's cell phone rang.

Sherman got right down to business. "Who are you?"

"Someone who can help," Turrin replied.

"Help?"

"You're having problems with Marco Conte. He's a dangerous man."

"Who says I'm having problems?"

"Someone I know. Harry, I have good ears and I'm a listener."

A long pause. Turrin knew Sherman was still on the line because he could hear the background noise.

"Do you have a solution?"

"I do. I'll pull you out and get you clear," Turrin said.

"Is this some kind of sick joke?"

"I don't hear either of us laughing, Harry."

"Before I end this call, tell me what this is about."

"Someone is taking a gamble, Harry, and is in the right place to do that for you."

"*Here*? In Vegas? Are you trying to get me killed or what? Jesus, if Conte even sniffs I've been talking to you, I'm already dead."

"So stay ahead of the game, Harry. Make that jump before he decides he can't trust you any longer."

"This is crazy. You know who you're talking about? Why the hell am I even still on the line?" Sherman asked.

"Because you know what I'm saying is the truth, Harry. You're mixed up with a bad crowd. Be honest. You handle the money for Conte. You know the kinds of things he gets involved with using the casino as a front. Do yourself a favor and get out before Conte makes a move."

Turrin had no doubt that beads of sweat were sliding down the sides of Sherman's face, that his body was shivering and it wasn't due to the weather. The voice on the phone was telling him what he already knew. His days with Conte were numbered—and those numbers were already starting to fall.

"I'll be at the café tomorrow, Harry. We'll talk." The little Fed ended the call.

TURRIN WAS PLEASANTLY SURPRISED—and relieved—when Sherman crossed the café and took his usual table. After the accountant had ordered, Turrin stood and crossed the floor to join him. The man glanced up, his face registering slight alarm.

"I didn't think you'd show," Turrin said as he took the seat across from Sherman. "Good to meet you, Harry. I'm Leo."

Turrin waited as Sherman's coffee and roll were delivered.

"If you can't help me, Leo, this could be one of my last meals."

"You have a cell phone on you?"

"Don't they provide you with one?"

"It's yours I want. Take it out and place it on the table."

Sherman complied, watching as Turrin opened the back and removed the battery and SIM card. He dropped the items into his pocket.

Sherman stared at him.

"Calls can be traced. You could be tracked."

"So now what? I make smoke signals?"

Turrin took out a satellite phone and placed it between them on the table.

"Use this one," he said. "It's clean and can't be traced. My people can track you with the GPS that's installed. And it has my contact number. If we get separated, you can call me."

Sherman didn't touch the phone. He had a look on his face that told Turrin he was unsure.

"Okay, so you're here. What's going down?"

Sherman laid it all out, about the missing money, Sol Lemke and the deadline Conte had given him.

"He'll do it," Sherman said. "Conte has a simple rule. Do it to them before they do it to you. Old school. He believes in bringing the hammer down if he sees a problem. Right now he doesn't trust me any longer. Even if I found his missing money, the suspicion would still be there. He gave me a few days. I know I'm reaching the end of my rope here."

"You're right about Conte. He's a low-life thug, and he'll want you dead. No two ways about it. Come on board and I can set things in motion. We relocate you somewhere safe. New identity. New name. You can rebuild your life."

"It sounds so easy when you say it. I have family. A sister and her kids."

"We'll look after them, too. Harry, I won't lie. This won't be easy for you. A lot of things will change. Harry Sherman will disappear. You and your loved ones will get new identities. If you have any doubts, think of the alternative."

Sherman reached out, picked up the sat phone and dropped it into his pocket, knowing that "Leo" was right. He understood a man like Conte, knew the man's capacity for revenge, retribution. The man had no conscience. His instinct was tuned toward his own survival. Nothing else mattered to him.

"I have information you can use to nail Conte. I recently discovered it." Sherman told Turrin what he had uncovered. "Do what you've promised and I'll give it to you when I'm safe."

"Then let's get out of here," the little Fed said, pushing back his chair.

Sherman pushed his seat back and stood. He caught his foot on the leg of his chair and stumbled slightly. It was just enough to take him out of the trajectory of the slug that missed him by inches and slammed into Turrin. The impact shoved the Justice man back, his seat toppling and taking him with it. He hit the ground hard, blood spreading across his shirt from the hole high in his chest.

The other customers panicked as realization hit in the wake of the gunshot. They scattered, Harry Sherman among them, and two more people were hit as the shooter attempted to pin Sherman down.

By the time the first police cruisers arrived, it was over.

**2**

In hospital and under guard, Leo Turrin was slowly recovering from surgery to remove a slug from his chest. The bullet had clipped a lung and had lodged in muscle.

Family and friends had visited after hurried cross-country flights. Even Hal Brognola, Justice Department honcho and director of the Sensitive Operations Group, a secret antiterrorist organization based at Stony Man Farm, had shown up, then quickly departed.

Turrin had given his evidence to the investigating team from Justice. Now, in the silence of his room, staring unseeing at the walls, Turrin tried to make sense of it all. He had been involved in the world of crime and its attendant horrors for so long he imagined nothing could shock him, yet he still found himself drawn into the effects of such pointless violence. He had learned that several innocents had been killed, including two children. What made it worse: there was not a damned thing he could do about it.

He heard the door to his room swish open. The door closed and Turrin became aware of a presence.

Unobtrusive.

Standing silently beside the bed.

Before a word was spoken, Turrin knew who it was.

"We are going to make this right, Leo."

When he heard those simple words, the little Fed felt a degree of tension drain away.

"It's not going to be easy."

"It's never easy," Mack Bolan said. "But it's doable."

"It should have been straightforward, Mack. Sherman was ready to make a deal. A new identity for information on Conte."

"Why would he do that?"

Turrin took a breath as a surge of pain slashed through his chest.

"The guy was at odds with Conte. My contact in Vegas said the casino boss was getting more and more aggressive with everyone around him—running the organization as if he was some kind of untouchable. A few people vanished after they had committed some minor discretions. Conte was showing there was no place for mistakes in his organization.

"Sherman knew his time had come when he was accused of stealing money from the accounts. He knew Conte would come after him. He'd want Sherman's head on a plate. So he took the only option he could." Turrin took another slow breath. "When Sherman found incriminating information in Conte's files, he saved it on a flash drive. It was his bargaining chip. When we met, he told me he'd give us the data that would give us the go on Conte's organization. Now I'm not sure the information will be worth what it's already cost in lives."

Turrin asked for water and Bolan obliged. Bolan placed the plastic cup in his old friend's hand and waited as he sipped the water through a straw.

"Leo, if this is too much right now, we can leave it."

Turrin shook his head.

"We don't have the luxury of time. Sherman's out there on his own. The guy is in a bad place, Mack. He's an accountant, not a street soldier. I contacted him and offered my help. Now he's on the run. Conte's kill squads will be hunting him. If they get to him first, it's over."

"Then we stop Conte, Leo. Play him at his own game. By the rules he sets down."

"Read up on him, Mack. This guy runs his organization through violence and intimidation and doesn't give a damn about anyone. The casino is his legitimate cover for what goes on behind the scenes. From what we've learned that's a hell of a lot."

"Justice knows but can't touch him?"

"Conte has the backing of his people out east. The real power is the Russian mob out of Brighton Beach. They have high-priced lawyers and money to burn on payoffs. These people know how to buy their protection, Mack. Justice has been trying to find a way in, but these guys have it sewed up tight. Sherman's information could go a long way to bringing them all down. But right now I have no idea where he is or what he's done with the evidence."

"The thing about sewing things up is the opportunity to pick at the stitches," Bolan said.

Those few words told Turrin that he could rest a little easier.

Mack Bolan was on board.
The Executioner was ready to roll.
Conte and the Russian mob were in for a rough ride.

**3**

"Marco, it's a call for you," Milo Forte said. "I think it's Harry Sherman."

Conte took the phone. "Yeah?"

"You double-crossed me, Marco," Sherman said without preamble. "I valued your word. I should have known better."

"Harry, it's business. Nothing personal. I have to go with the percentages and they were telling me I should cut my losses."

"You think? Marco, I might have had respect for you a while ago, but you just proved what a cheap hood you are—"

"You can't talk to me like that, you fucking bean counter. You know who I am?"

"I know *what* you are, Marco. A scared little gofer who has to jump through hoops every time your Russian boss says so. And right now you're in trouble. Bulova isn't going to be happy you let nine million slip through your fingers. I would have stuck to my agreement, but you couldn't even do that."

The silence was thick enough to cut.

"Where are you, Harry? Tell me so I can come rip your throat out."

"I would have helped, but now I'm going to do my best to see that you and Bulova go down. I have the goods on you, Marco. I found your hidden files. The ones that have all the names and dates and payoffs. I made a copy and I'm going to give it to the Feds. You just *had* to send out your guy with his gun to put me down. The trouble is, he screwed up. He missed me but hurt other people. So to hell with you all. You made me angry, Marco, and it takes a lot to do that, you loser."

"We'll find you, Harry, and I'll make it my personal business to cut you into little pieces."

The phone went dead in Conte's hand.

"Milo, that piece of garbage is threatening to hand over files to the Feds. Goddamn it, we need to find him fast or we're done."

VITALY DANICHEV SAT in the rear of the SUV, making no move to climb out. His driver sat patiently at the wheel, staring out through the windshield. He knew better than to disturb his employer when he was in such a mood. Tibor Kolchak flanked the driver. Even though he was Danichev's chief bodyguard, the huge man understood when to remain nothing more than a passive observer.

"All right, Tibor, let's get this done."

Kolchak climbed out of the SUV and moved his bulk to Danichev's door, opening it so that his boss could step out. He headed directly for the casino's entrance. Despite his powerful size, Kolchak stayed ahead of his boss, yanking open the door for him. Danichev walked inside and along the carpeted floor. Even at this time of day the casino was busy with people moving in and out. A constant stream of potential winners and losers.

"Mr. Conte is waiting for you in the Crater Lounge, sir," said the floor manager.

He led them through the casino to a closed door at the far side of the opulent gambling floor. They stepped through the door and into the semi-lit area of the lounge. The empty dance floor was surrounded by tables and chairs, and a long, curved bar sat at the rear. The motif of the room was of planets and stars, the ceiling illuminated by simulated lunar craters and subdued light.

Marco Conte sat at the bar on a high stool, two of his hardmen close by. His gaze settled on Danichev and remained there as the Russian approached. Conte had a drink in his hand and a cigar in his mouth. He was putting on an act of nonchalance, a display for Danichev's benefit. It was a wasted effort. The Russian ignored it.

"Have you found him?" Danichev asked.

Any form of greeting Conte might have been considering faded fast.

"No."

"And so you sit there doing nothing?"

"I have my people out looking for him," Conte said.

Danichev's lips curved into a faint smile a second before he exploded with rage.

"You have people looking for him. What the fuck does that mean? This accountant has run out on you. And you have done nothing to stop him. The Feds want him to give them this evidence he found."

Danichev began to speak Russian, his rage filling the room as he subjected Conte to an intense verbal rant.

His hands lashed out, knocking the cigar and the glass from Conte's hands.

The casino boss took the verbal assault without protest, his shock at being so intensely attacked rendering him speechless. He might be the head man in Vegas but under Danichev's intense rebuke he could have been a street soldier with no rank. He had heard about the Russian's powerful presence, but this was the only time he had been on the receiving end. He was physically trembling, his face bloodless; he realized his position so he remained silent. The last thing he needed to do was to offer some lame excuse.

"Get me a drink," Danichev said to Kolchak, suddenly reverting to English.

Kolchak stepped behind the bar. He sought out a bottle of expensive vodka and filled a tumbler, handing it to Danichev. The Russian savored the liquor before taking a swallow.

"At least this delivers as it should," he said after the vodka slid down his throat. "Pour one for Marco. I think he is going to need it."

Conte took the offered drink without protest. He hated the stuff, preferring a good malt whiskey, but at that moment he wasn't going to do anything to upset Danichev further.

"Get rid of the monkeys," Danichev ordered.

Conte dismissed his bodyguards. He was aware of Danichev's scrutiny, so he took another swallow of the vodka.

"So," Danichev said in a more conversational tone that did little to make Conte feel any better. "I got angry because you fucked up. You now understand how bad you fucked up. Because of your error the organization is now vulnerable to the Feds. The last thing we need is to be placed in their sights any more than we already are. Do you agree, Marco?"

"Yes. But we will find him."

"That is not the answer I was hoping for. What I asked was whether you think Sherman has left us in a vulnerable position."

Conte noticed that his hand holding the glass of vodka was trembling slightly. It angered him that Danichev could have that effect on him. And it annoyed him the way the man talked down to him.

In the seconds following his thoughts, Marco Conte realized his position, his power over events, was only granted by the ultimate heads of the organization. They wielded the big stick from their power base back east. His empire, out here in the sticks, only existed because it generated revenue—that ultimate power being demonstrated to him by the presence of Vitaly Danichev. If Danichev decided to end Conte's reign, he could do it simply by clicking his fingers and unleashing the hulking figure of Tibor Kolchak. It could happen in an instant and Conte would cease to exist.

"If he manages to hand over that information to the Feds, we could have problems," Conte conceded.

"Good. With that out of the way we must move to prevent this matter getting any further out of hand."

Danichev glanced at Kolchak.

The big man took out a cell phone that was dwarfed by his massive hand. He tapped in a speed-dial number and waited until the call was answered. He leaned across the bar and handed it to Danichev.

"Where are you?" the Russian asked. "Excellent. Come straight inside when you arrive."

TEN MINUTES and two more glasses of vodka later, Danichev heard the sound of raised voices. The doors to the lounge were pushed open and five men walked in.

"On time, as usual," he said.

The group was headed by a well-muscled man in his late thirties. His dark hair was close-cut, his angular face tanned, emphasizing the pale color of his eyes.

"Mr. Danichev," the man said, respect evident in his voice. His gaze passed over Conte before centering on Danichev again. "Ready to go, sir."

"This is Marco Conte," Danichev said. "He heads this territory for us. Marco, I want you to meet Anatole Killian. Anatole and his men are here to put right our little problem. I want you to give Anatole all the help he needs. He has my permission to ask any questions. To go through everything there is to know about our absent accountant. He has the full backing of the organization to do whatever is needed to resolve this matter."

Conte understood exactly what was implied by Danichev's words. He didn't need to have it spelled out any clearer. He knew exactly who Anatole Killian was. His team's reputation within the organization was well known, as was its purpose. He and his men were known as the Kill Squad.

"It appears that Sherman accessed sensitive data from Marco's computer and saved it to a flash drive," Danichev said. "That data, if handed over to the Feds, could prove extremely embarrassing to Mr. Bulova."

Killian considered what had been said. "Is this information that important?"

"Yes. It is Conte's master list of people, the amount of money paid to them, as well as the reason why it was paid and dates."

"I can understand why that kind of information is important," Killian said, "but how did Sherman manage to get hold of it?"

"Because he's a smart son of a bitch who managed to get into my secure files and access what was on them."

"Not so secure then," Killian said.

Conte emptied his drink. "So it fucking well seems."

"Anatole, don't upset Marco. He's not having too good a day."

"Sorry," Killian said. "Let me have everything on this Sherman. I need to find a starting point. Contacts this guy might have. Places he might go. Any family he might run to."

"Sherman has a sister and a niece. They live in Des Moines. A nephew is deployed overseas," Conte said. "We did a background check when he applied for the job. Apparently, Sherman and his sister don't really get on. The sister doesn't approve of his lifestyle. She believes Vegas is not the place to work."

"You think she is worried we might corrupt him?" Danichev asked.

"Something like that."

"If Sherman is on the move, he might contact his sister," Killian said. "Family loyalty."

"Have a local contact arrange for a home visit," Danichev said. "The sister might have what we need."

Killian nodded. "I'll get on it."

**4**

*Stony Man Farm, Virginia*

Aaron Kurtzman, the head of Stony Man's cyber team, propelled his wheelchair into the War Room and positioned himself beside Mack Bolan. In addition to the Executioner, Harold Brognola and Barbara Price, SOG's mission controller, were seated at the conference table.

The cyber wizards had been instructed to dig into Marco Conte's life and times. His background, the structure of his operations, the people he dealt with, his staff. All details had been entered into the Farm's supercomputer, logged and pulled into order.

Kurtzman's team had dug into FBI files, the records from ATF and police records. Even the legal firm Conte used to keep him out of jail had come under their cyber eyes. They had all that, plus the data that had been downloaded from Leo Turrin's files courtesy of Brognola.

Kurtzman began his presentation.

"The organization run by Marco Conte is ultimately responsible to the crime syndicate headed by Serge Bulova. Conte has complete control of *his* outfit, but at the end of the day he's part of the Bulova operation and anything that hurts Conte hurts Bulova. It seems that a recent task force investigation of Conte has made some inroads into his organization. Nothing that could stand up in court yet, but Bulova has been rattled by the interest shown in Conte's setup. That said, once news reached Bulova that there was a significant problem within Conte's organization, Justice intel says he sent Vitaly Danichev to monitor the situation."

"I've heard that name before," Bolan said.

"Danichev keeps people in line for Bulova. He's got a reputation as a no-nonsense enforcer. He gets results. The hard way, according to intel reports. Never gets his own hands dirty. There's a team of hit men who clean up any loose ends. They work under Danichev's control."

"Guns for hire?" Bolan asked.

Kurtzman nodded. "Unofficially they're known as the Kill Squad." He tapped at the slim keyboard on the table in front of him. A grainy image appeared on the large wall monitor, depicting a dark-haired man with an angular face and pale blue eyes. His hard features were clean-shaved and his expression was solemn. "These are the only pictures known to exist of the guy heading the squad and his second in command."

Bolan studied the face and committed it to memory. He would know the guy if he encountered him.

"Do we have a name?"

"Anatole Killian. That's all we've got. The other guy is Jake Fresco."

"Not the types you'd want to meet on a dark night," Price said. "Or even in broad daylight, for that matter."

"Do we assume Killian was behind the attempt to kill Harry Sherman?" Bolan asked.

"We don't know. The hit could have been set up by Conte. A sniper made the shot from a rooftop across from the café where Leo was meeting Sherman. You already know what went down. Sherman was on the verge of cooperating with Leo. He was ready to step away from the Conte organization and offer evidence that would give the task force enough to go for Marco Conte. Leo was going to give him protection."

"But the shooter made a mess of the attempt," Brognola said. "Hit Turrin instead of Sherman."

"He tried to clean up by taking more shots as Sherman ran," Kurtzman said. "He just made things worse, killing civilians, including two children."

"I haven't forgotten about the loss of those innocents, especially the kids," Bolan rasped.

The deaths of the children would be in his thoughts for as long as it took to make things right. And he would. There had to be a reckoning for the indiscriminate slaughter of people who were merely collateral damage for a killer out to make a buck. Bolan would not forget those deaths.

Or the injury to Leo Turrin.

"What have you got on Sherman?" Bolan asked.

"Harry Sherman," Kurtzman said. Another image flashed onto the monitor. "Thirty-eight years old. Unmarried. Pure and simple? A money man. He ran the accounts for Conte. Kept track of all the cash coming in and never took a wrong step until nine million dollars disappeared. We don't have all the details, but it looks as if Sherman's the fall guy for someone snatching the money.

"Sherman has a sister, Gwen Darrow," Kurtzman went on. "She lives in Des Moines. She's a lawyer with her own practice in the city. She's a widow with two kids. Laura is in college. Carl is in the military. He's on active service right now."

He brought up a picture of a handsome woman with dark hair and hazel eyes. There were two more images. One of Darrow's son, Carl, in uniform, and one of her daughter, Laura, who was an attractive, younger version of her mother.

"Good place to start looking for Sherman as any," Bolan said.

"I'll make travel arrangements for you," Price advised, gathering her file and leaving the room.

"Aaron, will you download the intel you've gathered to my sat phone?"

"You'll have it shortly."

The meeting broke up after another half hour. Bolan made his way to the room he used when he was in residence at Stony Man and packed a bag. Then he dropped by the armory where he chose the weapons he'd need for the mission: a Beretta 93-R and several magazines loaded with 9 mm ammo. He also chose a .44 Magnum Desert Eagle, as well as a sheathed Cold Steel Tanto knife and holsters for both handguns.

He liaised with Price, who set him up with his travel pack. Jack Grimaldi, the Stony Man resident pilot, would fly him to Des Moines.

"Pick up your vehicle at the airfield," she said. "A Chevy Suburban is being delivered as we speak. Try not to return it to the rental agency full of holes."

"That's happened before?" Bolan asked with a grin.

"Take a look at our insurance premiums," Price quipped and then winked.

"You ready, Sarge?" Grimaldi asked.

"Let's move out."

As Grimaldi turned and headed for the door, Price leaned forward and kissed Bolan.

"Stay safe, soldier," she said.

*Outside Des Moines, Iowa*

GRIMALDI TOUCHED DOWN at a private airstrip a few miles from the main airport. The ace pilot had contacts across the country when it came to safe landing spots. He was friendly with a large number of independent operators and those contacts came in handy when he needed an out-of-the-way place to land. Grimaldi was a sociable man, and when he made friends, those friendships tended to be strong and long-lasting. It was no secret that many of his acquaintances were of the female variety. He was the land-based version of the sailor with a girl in every port.

Bolan took his carry-all and placed it in the rear of the Suburban. He stowed his 93-R and shoulder rig in the glove compartment, within easy reach. He placed the bag holding his other weapons in the trunk.

"I'll be here if you need me," Grimaldi said as Bolan slid behind the wheel and fired up the Suburban's engine. "Try not to cause trouble."

Bolan glanced up from logging Gwen Darrow's address into the navigation system.

"Do I ever go looking for trouble, Jack?"

Grimaldi grinned. "You said that with a straight face."

He watched as Bolan drove out of the airstrip and picked up the road for the city.

**5**

Cash Cushman was driving. His partner, Billy Riker, was slouched in the passenger seat, his blank stare focused on the scene outside. They were in a stolen van, taken from a parking lot a couple of hours earlier. Once the job was done they would abandon the van and pick up their own car, which they had parked a couple of streets away. The van was dark blue, with no company logo, and they had fixed false plates in place of the originals. Both men wore dark coveralls and ball caps, a simple enough disguise for what they had to do.

The hit had been set up quickly, with little time to make more secure arrangements. It was not the way they liked to do things, but a fast response had been ordered, so they'd had to improvise.

They drove through the city, staying well within the speed limit and locating the target house without difficulty. Des Moines was a city they knew well. For them it was a simple enough contract. Locate the target, get the information they needed and pass it back to the principal. It would net them a tidy fee. In fact it was a nice, easy job despite having to wing it.

The street was quiet. It was midmorning and most residents were at work. Only a couple of cars were parked in driveways as Cushman rolled along, counting off the houses until he spotted the target. A small red Volkswagen Beetle was parked beside the house.

Cushman slowed and made a turn, pulling up behind the Volkswagen. He shut off the engine, got out of the van and went to the rear where he opened the door and slid out a package and a clipboard. He made a show of checking the clipboard before dropping it back inside the van and closing the door. While he did that, Riker slid over to the driver's seat and sat waiting. Cushman carried the package and walked up the driveway, bypassing the Volkswagen and walking to the back of the house.

He barely glanced at the rear yard, moving directly to the back door and tapping on the glass panel. He waited and tapped again. He heard movement inside then, through the frosted glass, saw a blurred figure approach the door. The door was opened on a security chain and a young woman's face appeared.

"Delivery for Gwen Darrow," Cushman said, a friendly smile on his face. He juggled the package and used his left hand to pull a folded sheet from his pocket. "I just need a signature, miss."

"My mom isn't at home."

"You can take the parcel," Cushman said. He waggled the sheet of paper. "I just need you to sign, is all."

The young woman hesitated then eased the door closed so she could remove the chain and open it wider.

"Mom didn't say anything about a delivery."

Cushman gave a shrug. "I don't know about that. I just deliver what I'm given."

He offered the package. The young woman, wearing shorts and a T-shirt, hesitated for a few seconds before taking the package. She moved back into the kitchen to place the package on the work surface and turned to go sign the delivery sheet.

Cushman had already stepped inside and had closed the gap between them. He had pushed the sheet of paper back into his pocket, producing a knife that he held out at the young woman.

"What are you—"

Cushman grabbed her arm and moved her from the kitchen and through open French doors that led to a family room.

"Hey," she snapped, "I don't know what you want but—"

"I want you to shut your mouth until I tell you to speak," Cushman ordered. "I ask a question, you answer. Tell me what I want or I'll cut your face to ribbons."

The young woman stood there, silently defiant.

"Okay," Cushman continued. "Where's your uncle? Harry Sherman."

GWEN DARROW LIVED in a town house in West Des Moines. It was a nice area. Big houses on a pleasant residential street. Mack Bolan cruised by the Darrow residence. It was late morning when the soldier made his pass, noting that the majority of drives were devoid of cars; at this time of day most people were already at work. He circled the area, also noting the absence of vehicles parked on the street. Bolan fixed the address in his mind and drove on.

A quarter mile down the road the residential area gave way to a small shopping mall. Bolan drove the Suburban onto the rooftop level of a parking garage and eased the vehicle into a vacant space. Turning off the engine, he retrieved his weapon from the glove compartment. He donned the shoulder rig and checked the Beretta 93-R, then shrugged on a leather jacket, knowing it would conceal his weapon. After securing the SUV, Bolan made his way out of the mall and retraced the route to the residential area. He moved at a steady pace, observing his surroundings.

The Darrow place was a couple of houses away when he saw the blue van parked in the drive behind a red Volkswagen Beetle. It had not been there when he had passed by earlier. The panel van had no company logo on its sides. Bolan took out his sat phone and called Stony Man. He wasted no time on small talk, simply quoting the van's plate number and asking for a vehicle check.

He got a call back minutes later.

"The plates are from a stolen vehicle," Kurtzman told him, "taken six months ago. They're from an SUV. Not a panel van."

Bolan put his phone away and increased his pace, his hand sliding inside his jacket and easing the 93-R from shoulder leather. He flicked the selector to single shot.

The Executioner had spotted the silhouette of a man sitting behind the van's wheel and kept him in mind as he moved up the driveway. The side of the house was on his right, a privacy fence on his left cutting him off from the neighboring house. Bolan was halfway along the side of the house when he picked up the sound of footfalls coming up behind him.

Bolan allowed the guy to get within a few feet before he came to a sudden halt and turned to face him. The move caught the guy by surprise. He wore coveralls and had a pistol in his hand. He made a halfhearted attempt to pull it into firing position. Bolan raised the Beretta and slammed the weapon into the guy's exposed throat. The impact stunned him, his eyes bugging open in shock. He stumbled back against the house, offering no resistance when Bolan snatched his pistol from his hand. The gunner clutched at his throat, choking as his crushed larynx restricted air flow. Then he slumped to his knees.

Bolan pulled a pair of riot cuffs from his pocket and tightly secured the guy's wrists and ankles, rolling him off the driveway and into the shrubs lining the fence.

He stuck his acquired pistol into his web belt then continued to the rear of the house, emerging onto a paved patio. The back door, which was open, led into a large kitchen. There was also a set of French doors that gave access to what seemed to be a family room.

Bolan recognized Laura Darrow from the photo Kurtzman had displayed.

A man in a pair of coveralls had his back to Bolan. The guy had a long-bladed knife in his right hand and was using it to make threatening gestures at the young woman. As Bolan quietly entered the kitchen, he picked up the verbal threats, too. Almost as an aside he noted the stubborn expression on Laura Darrow's face, caught the defiance in her voice as she answered back.

"…haven't seen my uncle for months. And even if I had, I wouldn't tell you…"

Bolan crossed the kitchen and moved through to the family room.

The attacker swung the knife back. As his right arm reached the apex of his swing, Bolan grabbed his wrist, yanking him off balance and kicking him behind a knee, taking him to the floor. As the guy went down, Bolan kept a solid grip on the wrist, twisting it hard until he heard bone crack. He raised the Beretta and slammed it across the guy's skull. There was enough force behind the blow to lay the guy out on the carpet. Blood seeped from the deep gash in his head. Bending over the unconscious man, Bolan secured him with plastic cuffs as he'd done to the first guy—wrists and ankles.

"What the hell is going on?" Laura Darrow shouted.

Bolan held up a warning hand. "Later," he said. He took out his sat phone and punched in the number for Barbara Price's direct line. When she answered, he gave her a quick rundown on the situation.

"What do you need?" she asked.

"There are two perps at Gwen Darrow's home that need to be taken care of as soon as possible. Only Darrow's daughter was at home."

"What about Laura?"

"She's unhurt. I'll keep her with me for now. I need to locate Gwen. She might be next on the list."

"I'll tell Hal and alert the local PD," Price said. "I assume the men are immobile?"

"I cuffed them both. The one in the house may have a broken wrist, so send medical help, as well."

"On it."

Laura Darrow was in his face the moment Bolan ended his call.

"Yes, well…" she said, "I guess I should say thanks for what you did. But what is this all about? Guns.

Knives. Why do these guys want my uncle Harry? Has he done something wrong?"

"Let's get out of here," Bolan said. "Do you need a coat? Your purse?"

The young woman stared at him for a moment then shook her head, turning to cross the room. She picked up a shoulder bag and a windbreaker.

"Okay? You want me to bring pajamas and a toothbrush, too? Maybe a book to read?"

Bolan almost smiled at her feisty attitude. It was evident Laura Darrow wasn't the kind to rattle easily.

"We need to move, Laura."

Bolan led the way out of the house.

She glanced at the secured guy on the side path as she stepped around him. "Any others you haven't mentioned?"

"No."

She followed Bolan as he retraced his route to the mall.

"Don't you have a car? Are we going to take a bus?"

"I parked at the mall," Bolan replied. "I didn't want to draw attention."

"Really? You made quite an entrance back there."

"No choice."

"Was that man was going to hurt me?" Laura asked, keeping in step.

"He was."

They might have been a couple out for a stroll, having a casual conversation.

"Let's start again. You know my name. Who are you?"

"Matt Cooper."

"Who—what—are you, Matt Cooper? You didn't

want to stay around until the police came. That's curious, so…?"

"So we need to get to your mother. I didn't want to stay around and have to answer too many questions."

She turned to stare at him. "Nice try, but I think there's more to it, Cooper."

"You need to call your mother. Get her to meet us somewhere away from her office."

Bolan took out his sat phone.

"I have my own cell," she said, producing it from her shoulder bag.

"Give it to me," Bolan said. "It's important."

Laura swapped phones. She watched as Bolan opened the back of her phone and took out the SIM card. He snapped it in two, dropped the pieces in a trash can as they passed and then removed the battery.

"I can't believe you did that. You think my insurance will cover the damage?"

"Somebody might be listening in or tracking you."

"Look, Cooper, before we go any further you have to tell me what this is all about. And what it has to do with Uncle Harry."

"Call your mother first. Get her to leave her office and go somewhere public where we can pick her up. A place you both know without having to describe it over the phone. She needs to do it now. Without telling anyone."

"My God, you're serious about this. Tell me your code name isn't 007." Laura tapped in a number and waited until it was answered. "Mom, it's me. Laura. I want you to listen and do what I tell you. And no questions. Walk out of your office. Don't say anything to anyone… No, Mom, this is not a joke. Just do what I ask. Go straight to our favorite place in town. Don't say where, just go. I'll meet you there. Go. *Now.*"

She handed back the sat phone, took hers and stared at it for a moment before dropping it and the battery into her bag.

"You realize you've lost all my contacts, Cooper."

"Better than losing your life."

"Okay, mister, it's time you told me what this is all about. No more stalling."

"Tell me about your uncle."

"What's to tell?" the young woman said. "He's some kind of money man, an accountant. He handles business for some casino in Vegas. We don't see him much and he doesn't talk about his job when we do."

"Harry Sherman *is* an accountant," Bolan said. "The man he works—*worked*—for heads a local crime syndicate. Your uncle got into trouble with this man—Marco Conte. Around nine million dollars disappeared. It had nothing to do with your uncle, but someone framed him. He was marked for a hit, but the shooter screwed up. He didn't get Harry, but others were killed and injured. Your uncle took off and he's been missing ever since."

Laura missed a step then recovered and stopped. Her face pale, she stared at Bolan as if he'd sprouted a second head. "It has to be true," she said. "No one would have any reason to make up something like that. And the shooting in Vegas was on the news."

They reached the mall and Bolan led her through the parking garage and to the Suburban. Laura slumped in the passenger seat as he fired up the engine and drove to the barrier, paid the fee to the man in the booth, then drove out.

"Which way?" he asked.

Laura gave him the directions and Bolan merged with the traffic. Ten minutes later he pulled in at the curb across from a coffee shop on Mills Civic Parkway.

"She's there," Laura said. "At that sidewalk table."

"Let's get her in the car," Bolan said.

He made a U-turn and pulled up at the opposite curb. Laura climbed out and went to the woman Bolan recognized from the image Kurtzman had displayed. He saw Laura speak to her mother and point at the SUV.

Although Gwen Darrow appeared reluctant, she followed her daughter and they got into the rear of the SUV. Bolan eased away from the curb and merged with the traffic again.

"Someone had better tell me what is going on," Gwen said.

"Do you have a cell phone?" Bolan asked.

"Yes."

"Give it to Laura."

"Now, listen here…"

"Give me the phone, Mom. It's important."

Laura took the cell phone and repeated Bolan's actions. The broken SIM card was slipped out through the SUV's window; she gave the battery to Laura.

"That was—"

"Mom, listen to what Cooper has to tell you."

Bolan gave her the full story, with occasional comments from Laura, bringing the woman up to date.

"Are you all right?" Gwen asked her daughter. "You're not hurt?"

"Thanks to Cooper, here, I'm okay."

"But they came into our home? Threatened you? We should inform the police."

"Already done," Bolan said. "The men who invaded your home should be in police custody by now."

"So where do we go from here?"

"I can arrange it so you and Laura will have protection."

"You believe these people will try again?"

"Your brother is on the run. He's been targeted. The people looking for him don't give up."

"This is insane," Gwen said. "A short while ago I was at my desk working. Now I have to listen to you telling me my brother is being chased by gangsters and our lives are in danger." She stared out the window for a moment. "You know what's ironic? I don't have any idea where Harry might be. We don't talk very often and I certainly don't know who his friends are."

"I tried to tell that to the guy who came into our house," Laura said. "He said he didn't believe me. Then he started waving a big knife at me. If Cooper hadn't showed up, I might be dead."

**6**

Bolan drove them out of the cityscape and into the open countryside until he spotted a roadside diner. He pulled into the parking lot and escorted the two women inside to the diner.

They took an empty booth and let the waitress fill their cups with coffee. Bolan could see both women were trying to come to terms with the revelations about Harry Sherman, so he allowed them time.

"They do say that sometimes it's the people close to you who can be strangers," Gwen said. "Harry and I had times when we didn't get on. There were harsh words, too."

"Mom, Uncle Harry can be difficult but you don't hate him."

Gwen smiled at her daughter. "There was never hate. Just a clash of personalities. Harry was never one for the conventional life. He could have had his own accountancy business, but after working for a number of

companies he chose what he considered a more excit-
ing challenge."

"Working for a casino?" Bolan ventured.

"Yes. Harry thought working in Vegas, with all
the gambling, the excitement, would give him what
he wanted. He saw it as something glamorous. I was
never convinced. You hear so many stories about that
kind of place."

"In some instances," Bolan said, "those stories are
true."

"This Marco Conte…" Laura began. "He's a criminal?"

"He works for a syndicate back east headed by a man
called Serge Bulova."

"A Russian?"

"Not a nice guy," Bolan said. "It appears Harry stumbled onto what goes on behind the scenes. To Harry's
credit he talked to the Feds, tried to work a deal in exchange for protection from Conte. That was when the
shooting incident took place. Harry was lucky. He got
away."

"But others didn't," Gwen said. "Am I being selfish
when I say I'm glad Harry wasn't hurt?"

"No. He's your brother. You feel for him."

"Cooper, can you help him?" Laura asked.

"If I can find him."

"I haven't seen Harry for almost eight months,"
Gwen admitted. "We were having one of our separa-
tions. I didn't call him, he didn't call me. I guess we
were both stubborn. I was always going on at him to
get out of his job at the casino."

Laura listened but didn't say anything for a while.
She pulled her coffee mug close to her face, eyes down.

Bolan noticed her attitude and suspected she was doing some thinking, wanting to get her facts straight before she spoke.

"Mom, you remember that man Uncle Harry used to talk about? The one he was in the service with?"

Gwen took a moment to recall the person. She nodded. "Justin… Ben Justin."

"Yes. A weird kind of guy. He only ever talked to Uncle Harry if he called on the phone. We've never actually met him," Laura told Bolan. "Harry used to fix up visits with Ben. He has some place out in the back country. Pretty isolated. He likes to be on his own. It's in upstate Nevada near a small town… Callisto. That's it. Callisto."

"Harry said he liked going out there because it was so different from Vegas. Quiet, with no blazing, no glaring. It was somewhere he said he could clear his head," Gwen said. "Do you think…?"

"It's worth a look," Bolan told her. "First, though, we get you two settled."

Laura stared at him. "This is bizarre, Cooper. A few hours ago we were fine. Now we're going to be hiding like fugitives."

"I don't suppose we have a choice," Gwen stated.

Bolan had his phone in his hand again. "For now there's no other way," he said. "These people won't give up looking for Harry. They'll see you as a way to get to him. So we take you out of the picture until this is all over."

"But what about work? People will want to know where I am. I can't just drop out of sight and—"

"Your disappearance will be handled. These things happen. There are procedures in place. Once everything is settled you can go back and pick up your lives," Bolan said. "But until we know it's safe, you and Laura are going to have to stay below the radar."

"If I refuse to cooperate?" Gwen queried. "You can't force us to run and hide."

"No, I can't," Bolan admitted. "The choice is yours to make. If you want, I can drive you back home right now."

Laura reached across the table and gripped her mother's hand.

"We have to do what Cooper says, Mom. I know it's not what cither of us wants, but believe me, if you'd been there when that man was in the house… Mom, he said he was going to carve up my face. You really think I want to go through something like that again?"

Gwen took a long breath, squeezed her daughter's hand and turned back to Bolan. "All right, Mr. Cooper, we'll do it your way for now. Until this matter is settled. When it is, we are going home."

Bolan made the call.

"We need to get Gwen and Laura to a safe place," Bolan told Price. "Put them somewhere temporary until a secure house can be arranged. Have Aaron run a check on a spot in Nevada. A town called Callisto. Looks like an old buddy of Sherman's lives out that way. It's worth a look. Call me back when you have things fixed… Okay, we'll wait. Make it fast. I need to find Sherman fast."

"Do we have time to eat?" Laura asked. "I'm hungry."

"Why not?" Bolan said. "We might not get time later on."

**7**

*Las Vegas, Nevada*

"This fucking mess is getting out of hand," Anatole Killian said. "Two of my men are in lockup and the sister and her daughter have disappeared. Is it me or have we suddenly become a bunch of amateurs?"

"These things happen," Jake Fresco said.

Killian turned on him, his face darkening with anger. "No. These things do not happen. I thought we were professionals, Jake. Maybe I've had it wrong all this time. Look at that cluster fuck Luca created. All he had to do was shoot Sherman and this would have been over. He screwed up the shot and then went crazy trying to make up for it by firing wild. Did you forget the result already?"

Fresco shook his head. "At least Luca got clear."

"So that makes it okay? *Luca got clear.* Where is he? Hiding under the fuckin' bed, ashamed to show his face?"

"He went to the local safe house."

"It won't be safe when we get there." Killian gathered himself, taking a couple of deep breaths. "Jake, get a team together. Go on the hunt for Sherman's sister. I have a feeling she could put us on track to find that little shit. I have to go talk to Mr. Danichev. Now there is a man who won't be happy with the way things are going."

Killian followed Fresco out of the room. He took a long walk through Conte's spacious ranch-style house until he reached the room where Danichev would be waiting. He tapped on the door, heard the summons and went in, closing the door behind him.

Vitaly Danichev sat behind the large desk Conte normally used. He was alone, framed by the wide window at his back.

"You want to sit down, Anatole?" he asked.

Killian stood at the desk, as relaxed as he could be considering the recent debacle, and waited for his employer to speak.

"We came all the way out here to show Marco how things should be run," Danichev said. "To say the least I don't believe we've made a good first impression." He paused. "At least you don't disagree?"

"No, sir," Killian said. "A poor start."

"Tell me you have your team on the move."

"Yes, sir."

"Anything on your two men?" Danichev asked.

"Legal is working on getting them out," Killian stated.

"So I gathered when I spoke to them."

"Our people won't tell the cops anything. We can resolve this in time."

"Time is something we're a little short of, Anatole. Bear that in mind. Getting our hands on Sherman is vital. He's ready to talk and from what Conte tells me, he has data that could hurt us all the way back to Brighton Beach. Right now there are a number of people with warm collars getting tighter every day."

"I understand the urgency, sir."

Danichev leaned forward. "As you said, Anatole, a bad start. Let's put it behind us and move on. No need to mention this again."

"Thank you, Mr. Danichev."

"Just one thing. When I spoke to the head of the legal team, he reported that our people at the Sherman house said they were attacked by a man on his own. Very proficient. Very fast. He seemingly came out of nowhere, took down our people and spirited away with Laura Darrow. Follow up on that."

"Consider it done," Killian said.

*Brighton Beach, Little Odessa*

SERGE BULOVA SAT UPRIGHT, his face rigid. His right hand rose, finger pointing. Every man in the room imagined it was pointing at *him*.

"You listen to me," Bulova said. "This is not a game. It is real. As real as it gets. If we do not take control, we will all go down. Every last one of us. Me included.

"This organization we have so carefully built will fall apart if that goddamned Sherman hands that information to the Justice Department. It will blow us into little pieces.

"I want your people on the streets. I want them covering the fucking country if the need arises. Find Sherman. I want him dead and I want that data in my hands so I can see that it is destroyed. Use everyone we have. Every contact, every informant. Make them talk. Cut out their hearts if they try to hold back. This has become a war for survival. Our survival. I don't give a damn about collateral damage. Anyone gets in the way, put them down. Whatever it costs." He rose from behind his desk. "I do not want to see any one of you back here unless it is to tell me you have succeeded. Let us get this mess cleaned up."

Bulova waited until the group had gone, then made a call to Danichev.

"Vitaly, you stay on Conte's tail. Watch and listen. He doesn't know it, but he's a walking dead man. It's down to that piece of garbage that all this has blown up. For the time being play along. Right now we need his local knowledge. Sherman is our priority. Find him."

"I understand, Mr. Bulova. Oh, we have located Luca D'Allesandro. He's hiding out in one of the safe houses here in Vegas."

"Not so safe for him," Bulova said. "All he had to do was put Sherman down. Not shoot up the town. Vitaly, that useless little shit has made things worse. Do me a personal favor. If you know where he is, give him my regards before you kill him."

AN HOUR LATER Danichev sent two of Killian's crew to drop in on D'Allesandro. Their information directed them to an apartment building on the edge of town. They entered the building and took the service elevator to the third floor. The apartment was at the end of the corridor, overlooking the street.

Joey Lombardi and Sal Benedetto pulled on thin

leather gloves as they stood at the door. Lombardi tapped on the door and waited.

"What?" D'Allesandro called out.

Lombardi identified himself.

"Time to go, Luca. Mr. Danichev wants you out of town. It's safer if you're not around until things cool off. Now open the door."

The sound of the chain being loosened was followed by the click of the lock. D'Allesandro stepped back as he opened the door to allow the two men inside.

He was lean and sallow-faced. His clothes were creased, his chin dark with stubble.

"I was starting to think you guys had forgotten me."

"We wouldn't do that," Benedetto said.

He glanced around the apartment. It was unfurnished. There was a sleeping bag in one corner of the living room and the remains of take-out food and drink.

"I brought that with me," D'Allesandro said. He gave a nervous smile. "You didn't bring any food with you?"

Lombardi shook his head. "No point."

"You don't have time to eat," Benedetto said. "Not where you're going."

Lombardi moved to face D'Allesandro. "No time at all, Luca."

D'Allesandro frowned, not entirely sure what Benedetto was saying.

Benedetto had quietly moved to stand directly behind D'Allesandro. He looked over the man's shoulder and caught his partner's eye. Lombardi gave the merest nod. Benedetto reached into his jacket pocket and brought out a black plastic tie, a large one already formed into a loop. He flicked it over D'Allesandro's head, sliding it into place around the man's neck. His right hand gripped the loose end, and he gave the tie a vicious tug, pulling it tight. The plastic bit deeply into D'Allesandro's neck. Benedetto added more pressure and the plastic sank even deeper, cutting through the flesh.

Blood began to ooze from the lacerations. D'Allesandro reached up to claw at the loop of plastic. It was so deeply embedded in his flesh that there was no purchase, but he would not have been able to do anything even if he had been able to get his fingers behind it. The plastic was too tough to be snapped.

D'Allesandro made harsh choking sounds as air was restricted by the encircling loop. He dropped to his knees, still digging at the plastic with bloody fingers. His eyes began to bulge in their sockets, tears streaming down his face.

Benedetto and Lombardi stood facing him, expressionless as they watched him fall to the floor, jerking in awkward spasms. The front of his pants showed a spreading wet patch.

"No point waiting around," Benedetto said.

"Hell, no," his partner agreed. "He's not going anywhere. I told him he had no time."

"Even fast food wouldn't have been quick enough for him," Benedetto said as he grinned at his partner.

They made a quick search of the room. The rifle D'Allesandro had used was in its case, leaning against the wall. Benedetto picked it up to take with him.

They moved to the door. By the time they stepped outside, D'Allesandro had stopped moving.

Benedetto closed the door quietly and they made their way to the elevator and descended to the lobby.

Outside the building Benedetto used his cell phone to call Danichev.

"He has your message," was all he said when his call was answered. "No problems."

"Get back when you can." Danichev cut the call.

"You want a coffee?" Lombardi said.

"Sounds good to me."

"There's a place just down the street. I saw it when we drove by."

JAKE FRESCO WAS outside having final words with one of the teams before they headed out. Killian joined him as the SUV moved away.

Fresco looked him up and down. "You look pretty unruffled for a guy who just has his ass chewed."

"It didn't happen, Jake. We had a friendly discussion about the current situation and I told Mr. Danichev we would take care of the problem."

Fresco grinned. "It must be love," he said. "So what next?"

"We keep looking. Cover every angle we can think of. His sister and the niece, they're family. I still think they're a good bet, but let's get some of Conte's local contacts to do some legwork. They know this town better than we do. Get them on the streets. Spread some money around. Jesus, Jake, this is Vegas. It lives on money. Let's use that.

"Somebody has to have something on Sherman. Find out what it is. We need it. Danichev might not be so forgiving if we keep coming up empty. At the end of the day it's his neck on the block as much as ours if we screw up again."

Fresco understood that. If things got too far out of

control and the head guys back east tired of the waiting game, it would come down on them. The top guys were known for their lack of patience and once heads started to roll the pecking order wasn't worth a piece of shit.

He only had to think back to how Harry Sherman had been dragged into the situation, even though it looked as if he'd been used by Lemke. Now he was on the run from the mob. A hunted man. He was no fool, though, Fresco decided. Sherman had made sure to gather insurance before he'd taken off. The information he had posed a threat to Conte and Bulova. It took some kind of guts to stand up to Conte. But when a man's life and family was being threatened, he was left with little choice.

Even a passive guy like Harry Sherman could stand up and be counted. Having Conte pissed off with him, and now Bulova letting loose the dogs, Sherman was a loose cannon. His resistance would not go down well with the top guys. They expected to be the ones dictating the action. Sherman had forced the issue and he was more or less telling the Conte and Bulova to go to hell.

However it turned out, Fresco decided, it was going to make things interesting for a while.

**8**

It had all been going fine until the front wheel hit a deep pothole. The sound of something cracking had reached Sherman's ears over the roar of the engine. The Jeep had lurched on for a couple of yards and had then kind of sagged on the right and started to make an unhealthy sound. He realized something had broken as he felt the vehicle pull to the right.

He stopped and sat for a moment with a feeling of dread washing over him. He switched off the engine, climbed out and walked around the Jeep to stare at the passenger-side wheel. It was canted at an odd angle. He was no mechanic. His skill extended as far as filling up with gasoline, maybe checking the tire pressure. But he knew the Jeep wasn't going anywhere.

Sherman remained staring at the crippled vehicle, aware of the hot sun on his back. He felt a rivulet of sweat slide down his face.

*This shouldn't be happening.*

It was not the way he had planned things.

Ben Justin's Jeep had been his ride out of the area to a place where he would catch the train to take him farther away once he hit Idaho and eventually over the border into Canada.

It was a plan born of desperation. After the horror of the shooting on the street, Sherman had figured even the Justice Department couldn't protect him from Conte and his enforcers. He had made his choice and he would go his own way. Tell no one. Do his best not to leave any kind of trail. He'd had no idea whether it would work, but he'd seen no other way for him if he wanted to stay alive.

Sherman had kept moving, stopping only to take money from a cash machine in a convenience store. He was aware that withdrawals could be detected, but he'd needed cash in his hand. There'd been a DHL franchise in the store and he had used the service to purchase a padded envelope. He'd slipped the flash drive inside, sealed it and filled out the required data. Paying the expedited fee, he'd handed over the package. With the flash drive off his hands for the next few days, Sherman had taken the next step: getting out of the city and heading for a refuge.

So he'd chosen to call on his old friend, Ben Justin. They went back a long way, had been in the military together. Even so, Sherman had been initially reluctant to ask for help. Justin had made it clear there was no problem and had volunteered to put him up for a few days while his friend worked out what to do.

Justin lived in a remote area, away from towns and people. The closest town was Callisto, a small blip in the empty Nevada landscape.

The solitary life appealed to Justin and allowed him the seclusion he desired. He had bought a section of land many years back and had built his home to his own specifications. He grew enough crops to feed himself and he asked for nothing more. He had the space, the silence of the landscape, and was not bothered by neighbors because the closest was almost twenty miles away. He needed little. The house was self-sufficient; Justin had his own generator to supply power, and he had dug a well that provided a fresh water supply. No radio. No TV. Cell phone coverage was thin but adequate.

Sherman envied his friend's contentment with his life. He could see the appeal for some—but it wouldn't have suited Harry Sherman for more than a short time. His problems apart, he had enjoyed his life in the casino. Life was always busy. It was noise and lights and atmosphere. He had found the occasional break from the hustle and bustle something he also enjoyed, and Justin always welcomed his friend.

Sherman had to accept that his life was about to change. His time in Vegas was lost to him. All he had now was a need to find a hideout. To simply try to stay alive.

It was hard to realize his old life was over. There was no going back. Marco Conte had seen to that. He had pointed the finger, set his dogs on Sherman's tail and wouldn't be satisfied until the man was dead, buried in some lonely spot where Sherman's secrets would die with him.

Well, to hell with you, Marco, Sherman thought. You'll have to find me first and I'm not going to make it that easy for you.

*Twenty-four hours earlier*

CALLISTO, THE SMALL TOWN where the bus dropped Sherman, lay in a shallow valley surrounded by an empty

Nevada landscape, a collection of time-faded and dusty buildings. Most of its inhabitants could have fit the description, too. Sherman trudged to the local coffee shop, where he ordered coffee and a hamburger and fries. When he had visited Justin previously, he had been in a car. Now he was on foot. When he asked someone how he could get to Ben Justin's place, he was told if he could wait a couple of hours a guy from the local store would be making a delivery out there. That suited Sherman fine.

The guy from the store was wrinkled and brown from a life under the Nevada sun. His truck looked to be as he was, but ran surprisingly well. Sherman sat beside the driver as they bumped and rocked along the dusty road. The old guy was not much of a talker, and Sherman gave up trying to make conversation after the first couple of miles. He sat back on the sagging-spring leather bench seat and studied the landscape.

It took them well more than two hours to reach their destination. Justin came out to meet them, staring at Sherman when he climbed stiffly out of the truck. He nodded hello and then helped the old guy to unload the supplies. As soon as that was done, the old man got into the truck, turned the vehicle and headed back to town, trailing a long stream of dust in its wake. Sherman helped carry the supplies inside.

"You want coffee?" Justin asked, showing no surprise at Sherman's unexpected appearance.

Sherman said he did and Justin made it. They sat facing each other across the kitchen table.

"You in some kind of trouble, Harry?" Justin asked.

"There's no fooling you, Ben."

"So, tell me."

Justin listened quietly, refilled their coffee mugs and considered what he'd been told before he spoke.

"It appears that high life you've been living isn't all it's been cracked up to be."

"Tell me about it." Sherman clamped his fists together so tightly the bones cracked. "I've been a damn fool all this time, Ben. Closing my eyes to what's been going on."

"So how do you plan to get yourself clear? Obviously, Conte isn't about to let things slide."

"I need to get across the border into Canada. Lose myself up there until I can figure out my next move."

"Why Canada?"

"It's a big country. There are lots of places where I can lose myself until I get it together. And I need to be somewhere waiting for a delivery."

"Okay. Next question. Why me? Now, don't take that the wrong way, Harry. You know you're welcome for as long as you want. I just can't figure out how I can help."

"You still got that old Jeep?"

"Around back."

"Does it run?"

"Yes. I don't use it much since I have the SUV, but she can still go some."

"I need to borrow it. I can use the back roads heading north into Idaho. From there I can pick up a local train to take me to the border."

"You serious?"

"Ben, I need to lose myself before Conte's crew finds me and increases my weight with a bunch of lead slugs."

"You're welcome to use the Jeep if that's the way you've decided to go."

"The farther away from Conte I get, the better I'll feel."

"Give me a couple of hours to check her out and you're set to go. Hey, you sure this is how you want to play this?"

"I'm sure."

"Harry, you look like you need to rest up. Make yourself something to eat if you want. Take it easy, pal."

Sherman moved into the living room and settled on one of the recliners. He let his head fall back. There was no use pretending. He did need to rest. He'd been on the move nonstop since leaving Vegas.

He closed his eyes, remembering how his world had come crashing down on him. Lemke had tried to shift blame onto him. If that hadn't happened, Conte would not have gone ape and threatened him.

But that was just it.

Conte *had* got mad…mad enough to put Sherman's back to the wall by ordering a hit—

Sherman heard a noise and sat upright, sweat beading his brow until he realized it was simply Justin working on the Jeep. He was reacting to every sound. Overcautious to the point of panic. If he wasn't careful, he would end up having a heart attack.

The thought brought a smile to his face. If that happened, Conte would be the one smiling: his problem over. No more Sherman, no more interference from the Justice Department. The perfect solution.

Let him believe that, Sherman thought. Because when I hand over those files he won't feel like smiling, the back-shooting son of a bitch.

# 9

Bolan had left his rental 4x4 in a shallow draw a couple of miles from Ben Justin's place. Armed with his Beretta and Desert Eagle, he had taken a circuitous route, coming up behind the house and spotting the two vehicles parked there. A dusty SUV bearing local plates stood next to a late-model Yukon. The high-end SUV might have been coated with fine dust but it looked too new to be anything but a rental.

It seemed likely that Justin had visitors—and not locals.

Bolan closed in on the pair of vehicles. A quick glance at the SUV identified it as a rental thanks to the sticker on the windshield.

Crouching beside the vehicle, Bolan spotted movement as a man stepped into view near the rear of the house.

It was the squat, black subgun the guy was carrying that alerted Bolan. That and the subdued but noticeable sound of someone in pain coming from inside the house.

Bolan stepped around the side of the house, moving quickly and silently, coming face to face with the gunner he'd spotted. The guy jerked the muzzle of his weapon in Bolan's direction as he laid eyes on him. He wasn't fast enough because Bolan had been expecting the confrontation. He slapped aside the guy's gun hand and followed up by punching a hard fist into his adversary's exposed throat. The soldier put his weight behind the blow and the guy began to choke as his airway was crushed.

He forgot about the subgun. Bolan did not. He caught the gunner's wrist, gripped and twisted against the bone until something snapped. His opponent would have screamed if he had been able to; all he managed was a raspy groan. Bolan forced him to his knees and drove his right knee hard into the guy's face. His head snapped back under the impact, the back of his skull hitting the wall behind him with force enough to shatter bone. As Bolan snatched the subgun from limp fingers the guy dropped facedown, blood pouring from his head.

"Hey!"

Bolan dropped to one knee, the acquired weapon in his hand rising on line. He saw a second man approaching from the front of the house, hauling a weapon from beneath his jacket. Bolan extended his arm, snap-aimed and triggered a fast burst from the subgun. The slugs punched into the guy's chest. He kept his forward motion for a couple of yards until his legs went out from under him and he slammed to the ground.

The Executioner moved forward, sliding around the corner of the house and entering the open front door. He could hear voices coming from the far end of the hallway as he barreled inside, heard the slap of footsteps as his presence was realized.

An armed man crashed through the door at the end of the hallway, spotting Bolan and opening fire. He carried an MP-5 and made the fatal mistake of firing it single-handed. The weapon spit flame, the muzzle rising as it fired.

Bolan came to a stop, his subgun held steady, and delivered a burst that caught the shooter mid-chest. The guy simply crumpled and dropped to the floor.

Casting aside the borrowed subgun, the Executioner unleathered his Beretta 93-R, the familiar pistol slipping comfortably into his big hand. He set the fire selector to single shot.

Bolan covered the distance to the door and went into the room fast. He dropped to a crouch, breaking to one side, his keen eyes taking in the layout.

The room had two occupants.

One was on the floor, blood pooling around him from multiple wounds to his half-naked body.

The other guy, bloody knife in his right hand, twisted, reaching for the pistol tucked behind his belt.

Bolan's 93-R tracked him and fired as the guy made his move. The 9 mm slug found flesh, the knife man flinching under the impact. The Executioner hit him with a second shot, a kill shot, and a spurt of blood erupted from the guy's shattered skull.

The echo of Bolan's shot faded as he crossed the room, kicking the discarded gun and knife aside before he crouched beside the figure spread out on the floor.

"Justin?" Bolan said.

His words barely registered; the man simply stared

at Bolan. His naked torso crisscrossed by savage knife cuts, blood running in bright streams from the incisions.

"Ben Justin?" Bolan asked again.

The bloodied man flinched, dragging in breath as pain coursed through him. Then his gaze centered on Bolan. It was as if a switch had been thrown and he was suddenly aware of his surroundings.

"I'm Justin."

Bolan took out his sat phone and made a call to Farm. Barbara Price picked up.

"Barb, you need to call in medical aid for Ben Justin. The guy's in a bad way. Somebody used a knife on him to get information on Harry. You'd better inform the local law—there are some fatalities. I'm guessing they're part of Conte's crew on the lookout for Sherman."

"We have the location," Price said. "I'll get right on it. Anything on Sherman?"

"Not yet."

Bolan ended the call.

"I told them…where Harry was…headed," Justin rasped, his voice fading to a hoarse whisper. "I couldn't hold out. The pain was…"

"Help is on the way. Don't worry about what you told them."

A hand that dripped blood reached out to grip Bolan's wrist. Justin's head rolled to the side so he could see Bolan clearly. "I didn't want to give him away. But I gave in… Jeezus, it hurts so much"

"I'm here to help Harry," Bolan said. "I need to get to him fast. Ben, where did he go?"

Justin began to talk, his words coming slowly, fading, and Bolan had to lean in closer to catch what the man was saying.

When Justin lapsed into silence, Bolan rose and went in search of the bathroom where he grabbed towels. Returning, he knelt beside Justin and used the towels to pad the bloody wounds. The wounds were severe but from what Bolan could work out no arteries had been cut. The cuts had been applied to make Justin speak, not to kill him outright. The blood loss was bad, but he hoped not life threatening. He stayed at Justin's side, talking quietly to the suffering man until help arrived.

THE MEDICAL TEAM, who flew in by helicopter, took over and did what they could to stabilize Justin before he was airlifted out of the area. Bolan had to deal with the local cops who had arrived in a police chopper. It was obvious they had been prepared to find him on-site and, despite the presence of bodies, the involvement of a federal agency made a difference. Bolan sensed Brognola's hand behind the deal.

The local cop in charge, a bluff middle-aged detective named Reynolds, checked each body, making sure he didn't contaminate the individual crime scenes. When he was satisfied, he joined Bolan, who waited patiently in the kitchen.

"You say these guys were looking for this Sherman feller?" he said. "And he's on the run because…?"

"Sherman was the money man for Marco Conte in Vegas. Things went sour for him—he discovered Conte was into more than gambling and running numbers—and he saw the light. Sherman hadn't realized how deep his boss was in until he found computer files that incriminate Conte and others in rackets. Payoffs and protection for official names. Looks like Conte had some interesting names on his payroll. If those files get into our hands, there are going to be a lot of people in deep trouble."

"Which makes Sherman a target."

"When Sherman had a meet with a Justice agent, one of Conte's shooters tried to take him down. It was a botched shoot. Innocent people got hurt, including a couple of kids who ended up dead."

"I heard about that. So your man was already a target?"

"The moment he talked to Justice."

"But he got clear?"

"And vanished."

"How did you find out where he'd gone?"

"The mob made an attempt to force a member of Sherman's family to give him up. I walked in on that. I was given Justin's location as a possible place to find Sherman."

Reynolds shook his head, ran a big hand through his cropped graying hair.

"Are you in the habit of always showing up at the right time?" he asked. "Hell, not that I'm complaining. This guy might have ended up dead if you hadn't walked in."

"It doesn't always work out like that."

"Who are these guys you tangled with?"

"I'd guess a backup crew. Low-rent contract hoods sent to force information out of Justin. Conte's doing everything he can to find Sherman. He wants to get his hands on those files."

"So where do you go from here?"

"I'm going to pick up Sherman's trail. Try to get to him before Conte's crew does."

"Anything I can do to help?"

"Tell me how I get to this location." Bolan pulled a folded sheet of paper from his pocket and showed it to Reynolds; he had committed the details to paper after Justin had slipped into a semi-conscious state, not wanting to lose any of the information.

"Small town about thirty-five miles north. There's a spur for the main line that runs fifty miles along. If Sherman picks up that spur, he can ride until he reaches the end of the line. There are a lot of choices from there."

"Canada?"

Reynolds nodded. "That trail leads all the way up into Idaho, then across country until the border. You think that's where he might be heading?"

"Justin mentioned it before he passed out."

"Big country up there. Plenty of places somebody could hide out."

"I think that's what Sherman's planning. He probably needs to hide out before he makes his next move."

"Why hasn't Sherman sent the data to the Justice Department?" Reynolds queried. "He could have done it from any computer terminal."

"I don't think he has the data on him. I think he sent it somewhere he could pick it up once he figured he was safe. Since Vegas he's been on the move, unsure who he could trust."

"So you think he sent it on ahead? Mailed it to himself maybe?"

"Something like that."

"That's a hell of a risk," Reynolds said. "It could get lost. He could get himself shot…"

"Harry Sherman has been shot at, chased, his world turned upside down. The guy may not be taking time to figure everything out clearly. But he still understood the need to get that data away from Conte and his crew and didn't want to risk losing it altogether."

"Well, there's only one way you'll get the answer, Cooper. Find Harry Sherman, if he's still alive, and ask him."

"That's exactly what I intend to do."

BOLAN CALLED STONY MAN and got Price to patch him through to Aaron Kurtzman.

"What can I do for you, Striker?"

Bolan gave the computer genius his update on the situation. "I need to find Sherman before Conte's crew. He's using Justin's old Jeep. Any chance you can locate it?"

"From what you say, he wants to disappear and has no real plan. That makes it harder. Not impossible. Just harder."

"Yeah, but his buddy just told me where he thinks Sherman is headed. The thing is, he has a good head start and I can't count on the fact that Conte's people don't have the same information."

"The best we can do is a satellite scan on the area. Maybe pick up his vehicle. It's a long shot but worth a look."

"Any other ideas, Aaron?"

"We'll make a start and get back to you. First thing I need is a cup of coffee."

Bolan smiled to himself. "I would think that brew of yours more likely to jam up your brain."

"Hey, my coffee stimulates my thinking processes. Do not dis my coffee, brother. Anything else?"

"I'm thinking Sherman has mailed the evidence to himself. Most likely to an address in Canada and he would have done it before leaving the Vegas area. Can you run some checks to see if he sent anything out?"

"Hell, why don't you give us something hard to do," Kurtzman quipped dryly.

"I know, I'm asking a lot."

"I wouldn't expect anything easy coming from you."

"Any first thoughts?" Bolan asked, detecting the click of keyboard keys across the line.

"I'm thinking he'd avoid standard mail. More likely he'd pick one of the courier services, UPS, FedEx, DHL. We'll run checks on last-day dealings. We have his home address and we have a possible destination. We'll track it down."

"Check with Gwen Darrow. Ask if she has any thoughts on a location in Canada Sherman might have a connection with."

"What do you need us for, big guy? You're almost there by yourself."

"I'll wait for your call."

After squaring away with Reynolds, Bolan left the area, picking up the road Sherman would likely follow as he headed upstate. En route, he contacted Grimaldi.

"Hey, Sarge, how goes the good fight?"

Bolan told the Stony Man pilot what had happened and where he was headed.

"I can cover that distance faster than you," Grimaldi said. "Do you want me to hit the sky and give you some backup?"

It took Bolan no time at all to reach a decision.

"Yeah, that works for me, Jack." He gave Grimaldi a description of the Jeep that Sherman was driving. "Just cover yourself. If there's a mob crew around, no heroics. Just watch and let me know."

"You got it." Grimaldi signed off.

THE HELICOPTER HAD already been fuelled. As he powered up the aircraft, Grimaldi scanned the references Bolan had given him and entered the information into the on-board GPS. The coordinates presented him with a flight plan. Grimaldi took off, reached altitude and set the chopper on course.

It was a clear day for flying. Grimaldi had an empty sky around him, with excellent visibility. He settled back and held his course. This was the Stony Man ace pilot's natural habitat. He felt complete once he was in the air. In his mind this was the ideal place to be. There was nothing better—he allowed himself some correction there; a pretty woman and a bottle of good whiskey came a very close second. If he could achieve and blend all three, he would be a happy man.

This day all he had was his helicopter and a clear sky, so there was little to complain about.

**10**

*Las Vegas, Nevada*

Overhearing Danichev's conversation with his man in the field gave Conte a lift. Not much of one but enough to give him momentary relief. Danichev's man had lost Sherman. Sherman had stayed ahead of them and, from the phone call and Danichev's reaction, continued to elude them. Conte could tell by Danichev's posture—hunched over the cell phone in his hand—that he was not pleased.

As much as he wanted to make a comment, Conte kept his mouth shut. He wasn't out of the woods himself yet and with the mood Danichev was in, the man would be ready to hit out at anyone who even slightly provoked him.

Sherman had screwed Conte over. He had taken off before Conte could deal with him, stealing information the Feds would drool over. And then along had come Danichev, flaunting his power and determined to impress Conte with his elite killing squad. But right now he had egg on his face. Sherman had given his hotshot enforcers the slip and left them with their dicks in their hands.

Danichev straightened and turned slowly to stare at Conte. Being in the gambling business meant Marco Conte had learned long ago how to maintain a neutral expression. He presented Danichev with a blank look.

"I imagine you're enjoying this, Marco. Your runaway accountant making my boys look stupid."

"Don't forget what he did to me," Conte returned. "You think I want him to get away with it?"

Danichev only grunted. He passed his phone to Kolchak, who began to speak to the caller, moving away from his chief. Danichev crossed to the wet bar and poured himself another large glass of vodka.

"You have fucking lousy luck with your employees," he said, "but you stock good liquor."

"So when you fire me I can get a job as a bartender," Conte said.

Danichev offered a wide, mirthless smile. "Don't you need working hands for that?"

Without a word Conte walked out of the room and made his way into the main casino area. It was not quite midday, but the place was reasonably busy. Conte stood and watched the milling players. He listened to the noise, saw the lights and, despite his current problems, allowed himself to be drawn into the ambience.

If he was going to lose all of this, he might as well enjoy it while he could.

One of the hostesses paused in front of him—a beautiful young woman in a skimpy costume.

"Would you like your usual, Mr. Conte?"

"Why not, Janice?" he said. Conte prided himself on knowing every one of the girls by name. "Thank you."

He watched her walk away and could not help smiling. If nothing else, he was a professional, keeping up appearances despite feeling sick to his stomach.

"Almost as good as the condemned man's last meal," Danichev said. He was standing at Conte's side.

"Whatever is going to happen, I can't avoid it," Conte conceded. "So do your worst, Vitaly, and stop playing Mr. Big. It's becoming tedious. I know I'm on a rocky road, so you making crap remarks isn't going to make me feel any worse."

Conte moved to meet Janice as she returned with his drink. It was a glass of his favorite whiskey. Rich and mellow, it came from his private stock. He held it up and toasted Danichev.

"To your health," Conte said as he walked away.

"Are you going to let him get away with that?" Kolchak asked.

"His time is coming, Tibor," Danichev said. "Allow him his moment of fun. Now, where are we with that little prick Sherman?"

Kolchak took a moment to reply. His thought processes were slower than most. He knew it, so he used the time to review what he was going to say before he did speak.

"There is no change," he said. "Killian has his people following Sherman. He is still a good distance away, but his friend Justin was persuaded to give up what he knew. They will find him."

"The rest, Tibor," Danichev said. "I can tell when you're holding something back."

"It could be nothing. Killian said they could not

make contact with the men he left at the Justin house. Perhaps there has been trouble there."

"Like the trouble at Sherman's sister's house?" Danichev asked. "Tibor, I don't like unexpected problems. Things that happen without apparent reason unsettle me."

Kolchak showed one of his infrequent smiles; it was an awkward gesture and his broad face took on a chilling expression.

"I know how to cure that," he said.

He walked away and went to the bar, returning with a thick tumbler filled with vodka. The tumbler was almost lost in his large hand.

"It is like having my mother following me around," Danichev said as he took the drink.

"I do not think your mother would give you vodka."

The cell phone in Kolchak's hand rang. He took the call, listening intently before he handed the phone to his boss, silently mouthing the word "home."

Danichev took the phone and raised it to his ear. When he spoke after a minute, he used Russian.

The man on the other end of the phone spoke in his Mother tongue. Despite having lived in America for many years, his English was poor. He was old style *Mafiya*, a man who refused to change his ways.

"I hear things are not progressing as quickly as expected."

"The situation here already existed," Danichev said. "It takes time to catch up with everything. The man, Sherman, had already fled when we arrived."

"Have you found out where he is?"

"We have learned that Canada might be his destination. Killian and his crew are on his trail. He has a good head start, which leaves us at a disadvantage. But we have people all across the area. We will find him."

"I am only interested in positive results."

"And I am not making excuses. Simply stating the facts," Danichev said sharply.

There was a pause on the line.

"Very well, Vitaly. Do whatever is necessary to conclude this business. Use whatever assets you need. There are people you can call on?"

"Yes. Killian is pulling in local assets."

"Expense is no problem. Remember that if this Sherman hands the information he stole to the Feds, the consequences could prove extremely embarrassing... *for all of us*."

"Understood."

"Keep me informed."

The call ended. Danichev stared at the cell phone for a moment then quickly drained his glass, feeling the vodka burn its way down his throat.

"He was not happy?" Kolchak asked.

"He was not happy. And unless we end this chase very soon, he will become even unhappier. Tibor, another drink."

The boss had not been pleased and Danichev's slightly irreverent comeback would not have endeared him to the man. There was a momentary regret then Danichev passed over that. It was all very well to be the old man sitting in comparative comfort back in Little Odessa. He expected everyone to obey his commands to the letter, allowed no setbacks, as if by simply snapping his fingers all problems would be easily solved. As much as he honored the old man, there were times when Danichev wished he would hurry up and pass on.

Serge Bulova was ancient, yet stubborn enough to hang on and rule as he always had, with an iron fist. He refused to acknowledge it was a different time. That ruling by sheer force and by the old ways was a thing of the past. Yet he was still revered, most likely feared, by those around him. His presence was enough to silence any dissent. He surrounded himself with his trusted coterie of bodyguards, men who had great loyalty and who would step into the path of a bullet for Bulova.

Damn you, old man, Danichev thought, why don't you die and let the new generation take over?

He took the glass Kolchak handed him, tasted the vodka and let it calm him. His thoughts about Bulova's longevity could wait for anther day. Right now he needed to concentrate on the matter at hand. Finding Sherman and dealing with him before he presented the Feds with his package of evidence. They would go to town if they did get their hands on it.

Danichev managed a bitter smile; the material Sherman had stolen could bring them all down in one mass. If that happened, getting rid of the old man wouldn't matter because once the dominos started to fall, they would all tumble.

"Tibor, make some calls. We need to recruit more local labor. Backup for Killian. And make sure Sherman's picture is sent to everyone's phone."

"Killian won't like that," Kolchak said. "He likes to play his own game."

"I'll handle Killian if he makes noises. I'll remind him who is paying the bills."

Danichev hoped Killian did voice his protest. It would allow Danichev to hit back, by venting his own anger on the man.

Expecting results, as the old man did, did not change the facts. Sherman was in the wind, and there was no miracle that would allow them to simply reach out and take him down. It had to be done by the numbers. Like it or not, they had to go through the motions, no matter how long it took.

Danichev drained his glass. He held it up, longing for more vodka. He resisted. This was not the time for weakness. He handed the empty glass to Kolchak.

"Coffee, Tibor. Strong and black."

**11**

Bolan swung off the narrow ribbon of road and onto the parking area beside the lone store and gas pumps. He turned off the engine, scanning the area as he climbed out of the SUV. He took a moment to ease the kinks out of his frame and examine his surroundings. Not that there was much to see: a small gas station on an empty stretch of rural highway. Flat terrain all around. No outstanding features.

In the far distance he could see an isolated farmhouse, a slowly turning windmill moved by the soft wind, and an expanse of fields, the sparse crops wilting under the hot sun. There was no movement out there. The road in both directions was empty, as it had been for the past few miles.

He heard the creak of a screen door and glanced over his shoulder in time to see a lean figure emerge. Wearing bib overalls, a plain blue denim shirt and a ball cap with a frayed bill, the man looked to be in his late sixties. Deep-set eyes in a weathered face roved back and forth, almost as if the guy wasn't comfortable in his own familiar surroundings.

Bolan sensed the first flicker of unease as the man approached.

The guy's eyes settled on Bolan and the expression on his face confirmed something was wrong.

Over the bony shoulder, behind the screen door, Bolan caught a shadow of movement.

The shadow pulled back out of sight, waiting for Bolan to step out from the cover of the SUV.

The Executioner caught the old man's gaze and held it. He moved so that he was directly in front of the man, hiding himself from anyone who might be watching from inside the building.

"How many?" Bolan asked quietly.

"Three."

"Armed?"

"Uh-huh. Like they're out to start a goddamn war."

"Get down. Get under the car. Now!"

The old guy moved fast for his age, his lean body dropping to the ground. He scrabbled forward, squirming beneath the bulk of the vehicle, and in the same moment Bolan moved quickly along the length of the SUV, skirting the rear, the Beretta 93-R slipping easily from the shoulder rig into his hand.

The screen door was kicked open. A gunman came out, subgun clutched in his hands. He raced toward the rear of the SUV, his finger curled around the trigger as he sought his target.

But he saw nothing.

The guy scowled. "Show yourself, asshole," he said. He took another step forward, dropping the muzzle of the subgun to the underside of Bolan's SUV. "Maybe I'll shoot the old bastard instead. I think he talks too much."

Bolan had dropped to a crouch, moving out of sight long enough to grip the 93-R in both hands and lean out from the back corner of the SUV. He tracked in and triggered a 3-round burst that punched into his target's body. The guy grunted as the 9 mm slugs hammered his midsection. He slipped to his knees, already forgetting about the weapon he was holding. His reflex action made him pull back on the trigger, the subgun drilling a burst into the ground.

Before the first guy had hit the earth, his two partners burst outside, the screen door swinging wide to slam against the outer wall.

The pair separated, one moving left, the other to the right. They both carried subguns and the closest guy started to fire as he angled in Bolan's direction. His shots were uncoordinated. A couple of 9 mm slugs creased the SUV's rear quarter panel. The guy was obviously not concentrating his fire. He'd assumed Bolan was still behind the vehicle even though he had yet to lay eyes on the man.

Still low, Bolan swung the Beretta and delivered another 3-round burst that blew the guy's right knee apart and dropped him. Screaming, the gunner slammed to the ground, the impact stunning him. He failed to see the Executioner as he leveled the 93-R and put a triburst into his skull, spreading a bloody mess across the hard-packed earth. He died not having seen his target.

Bolan moved instantly, knowing that the third guy, the one who had moved to the right, would be circling the SUV, coming around the front to take him on from the rear. A creative move but not smart enough to confound someone like Mack Bolan. The moment he had triggered the 3-round burst, the Executioner swiveled and pushed to his feet, moving to face the third would-be shooter. Bolan already had the Beretta on line as he slid around the rear of the vehicle. He picked up on the advancing gunner, who had chosen to move the length of the SUV, lowering his body to reduce his target area. It also forced him to lower his shooting stance so his subgun would have to be raised before he could fire.

Bolan had no such problem.

The second he stepped into view and confronted his adversary, Bolan acquired his target and triggered his pistol. Two 3-round bursts were fired into the gunner's head, the slugs blowing apart his skull in a flash of bloody flesh and bone. He went down without a sound.

Bolan kicked the weapons away from each body then checked the corpses for ID and other weapons. He found one handgun. None of the men carried identification. No wallets. Just cell phones. He noted they were all well dressed. The style of clothing told Bolan they were not locals. He snapped a photo of one of them to send to the Farm.

The old guy wriggled out from under the SUV.

Bolan went over and helped him to his feet. "Thanks for the warning," he said.

The man adjusted his ball cap. "Likewise," he replied. "I guess they weren't friends of yours?"

"No way. When did they show up?"

"An hour ago maybe. Just walked in and took over the place. Said if I wanted to see the sun rise tomorrow, I had to do what they told me."

"You took a chance coming out to warn me."

"Hell, boy, I didn't fight for my country to be scared

by the likes of them." The old man grinned. "Hell, we screwed them, son. You handled that pistol pretty good so I figure you done it before."

"Some," Bolan admitted.

"You a cop?"

"Not in the way you might expect."

"Fed? Undercover?"

"Close enough."

"So who were they?" the old-timer asked.

"Not cops," Bolan told him.

"I worked that out, as well, son."

"They were hunting for someone."

"I guess that would be the feller in the old Jeep that belongs to Ben Justin. He lives a ways back down the road. Right?"

Bolan took out his phone, brought up the image of Harry Sherman and showed it to the man.

"That's him. Nice feller. He filled up with gas."

"Did he tell you where he was headed?"

"Kelly's Junction. He was asking about train schedules."

"How far is it?"

"No more'n a couple of hours in that fancy gas guzzler of yours. That young feller in trouble?"

"Some. I'm trying to prevent it from getting worse."

"I figured that. So what next?"

"I call this in. Get help out here to take these guys away."

The old-timer shook his head. "And there I was thinking it was going to be just another quiet day." He rubbed his chin. "Hey, you still want gas?"

"Yeah, fill it up with the best you've got."

Bolan moved away and took out his sat phone. He gave Price the breakdown on what had just happened.

"These people sure are determincd," Price said. "Are you okay?"

"I'm fine. By the way, what about Leo? How's he doing?"

"He's coming along."

"Glad to hear that. Now, can you pinpoint my location?"

"Yes."

"Put out a call for the local law to come out and deal with this. Ask for Detective Reynolds. He was at Ben Justin's place. He understands the situation. It'll be interesting to find out who these people work for. I'll send you the photo."

"I though you said there were three of them. Should we expect multiple images?"

"Just the one," Bolan said, pressing a key on his sat phone.

"Why…?" Price paused. "Oh, I get it." She didn't ask further questions. There was no need.

When the transmitted image came through, Price immediately forwarded it to Kurtzman's team to run against their facial recognition program. The result was quick and Price was not surprised to find herself looking at a detailed and expansive rap sheet belonging to the now-late Vincent LaRusso. His career had been brought to an abrupt end the day he'd confronted Mack Bolan.

"Mack, you still there? I have confirmation on your photo. Vincent LaRusso."

The Executioner knew the man. His only jail time had occurred in his early twenties. He'd spent three years behind bars, suffered the expected indignities and come out the other side older but not necessarily wiser, although he'd obviously stepped into a job with Marco Conte's organization as an enforcer.

"You know him. He was a young Turk working his way up through the ranks—" Price began.

"Well, he isn't going to become an old Turk," Bolan said.

"You know, we have to work on your comebacks," Price said.

"Only if the lessons are private."

"That goes without saying."

"Deal, then."

"It sounds as if Conte's seriously upped the ante," Price pointed out.

"If Sherman can present his evidence, Conte and a lot of people are going to be doing hard time."

"If there are high-level names, those people are going to do everything they can to suppress evidence. Strings will be pulled so hard they'll make music."

"Then we make sure the evidence gets into the right hands. Don't worry. We can do it."

Bolan heard Price's sigh of frustration.

"They'll throw everything they have at you and Harry Sherman. I don't want—"

"Not going to happen, Barb. I'm taking this all the way down the wire. So quit frowning at the phone and just keep the faith."

"How do you know I'm frowning? Don't tell me—it's a gift."

"You know me so well, Ms. Price."

"It's a work in progress."

## 12

Danichev called Anatole Killian into his suite. He waved a hand in the direction of the wet bar.

"Help yourself, but make it a quick one."

"Sounds urgent," Killian said, pouring himself a shot.

"I just got the news. The US Marshals Service is moving the Sherman woman and her daughter to another location. That gives us time to set up an intercept. We're getting a second chance to get our hands on that bastard's family. Anatole, this might be our last shot, so don't let it be screwed up this time."

He handed Killian a note.

"Looks like your contact earned his money," he said after reading the details.

He took out his cell phone and hit a number. It was not a speech call, simply an alert for the guy on the other end to call Killian back, using a burner phone that would connect with Killian's. The return call came within a few minutes.

"Devonne, I have a job for you. This has to be set up fast. Use your best people." Killian read the details from the note Danichev had handed him. "We get one shot at this. It's important. Fuck this up and we could all be heading for the crapper. No second chances here. You've got four hours to make the location. We need the women alive. One of them at least. The escorts are expendable… Yeah, I imagined that would please you."

Danichev listened attentively as Killian went through the fine details then disconnected. It was, he thought, nice to watch a professional work.

"All set up. Devonne and his team will be on their way in the next thirty minutes."

"Good," Danichev replied. "Every penny we spend on our inside man is worth it."

"You think this will bring Sherman out of the woodwork?"

"Whatever else Sherman might be, he's not the type to abandon family. The minute that little shit finds out his sister and niece have been taken, he'll do anything to save them."

"You're sure of that?"

Danichev smiled. "I'm sure. Family ties tend to be strong."

"Nice to be sure," Killian said.

"Anatole, have faith. Aren't I always right?"

Killian drained his shot and twirled the glass in his fingers. "Sure," he said.

"I want you and Jake out there to deal with Sherman's family. No arguments, Anatole. Do it. Enough time's been wasted. This time, no mistakes."

You're always right, Vitaly, even when you're wrong,

Killian thought. He took the man's orders because that's what he was paid to do.

Despite knowing he was working with an accomplished team, and though the hit had all the marks of success, Anatole Killian still felt apprehensive. He knew how things could go off-line, how hits could turn around and snap back. So he wasn't about to chalk this up to done and dusted until it was over and they had Sherman's family safely locked away. Let Danichev congratulate himself. Killian would keep his congratulations on hold until there was no chance of it biting him in the ass.

With the previous lack of success, Killian reached a decision. Danichev ran the show, so he told Fresco to have their helicopter ready to take off. The standby aircraft would get them to a destination faster than any road vehicle.

"We going somewhere?" Fresco asked.

"Vitaly wants us there when they bring Sherman's family in. We need to get this almighty mess cleared up. It's time we made Sherman realize how deep in the shit he really is. I'm getting really pissed the way this number cruncher is running around and making us look stupid. Jake, get it organized."

**13**

"I thought this was where we would be staying until things were settled," Gwen Darrow said.

"This was never going to be permanent, ma'am," the marshal replied. "A hotel isn't the most secure environment. There are too many variables that aren't under our control. People are in and out all the time."

"And the room service menu isn't all that creative," Laura added.

The marshal smiled. He was getting used to her casual remarks.

"Good enough reason to move on, then," he said.

He was a tough-looking man in his early thirties. Good looking, too, in Laura's eyes. And, anyhow, she was ready for a move to somewhere less restrictive. The marshal's partner, older, was plainly the one in charge. He had the look of a professional cop. The man didn't talk a lot, but he was constantly on alert and both Laura and Gwen were more than grateful for the presence of both men.

"You ready to move?" the older marshal asked. "We'll go down the service stairs. The vehicle's parked out back. You go straight to it. No hesitation. Okay?"

"You think something might happen?"

The marshal, named Trenton, said, "There's always the possibility *something* might happen, miss. Our job is to try to anticipate it."

Laura offered a wry smile, obviously sorry that she had asked.

As they left the room, Carson, the younger marshal, patted her shoulder. "We'll get you there."

They reached the big, black SUV without incident. The marshals took the front, Carson at the wheel.

"Buckle up," Trenton ordered.

Minutes later they were heading out of the city, Carson driving them along a quiet back road. The urban sprawl began to drop behind them.

"How long until we get there?" Gwen asked.

"A couple of hours," Trenton advised. He took out his cell phone and reported in. "Transfer on schedule. No prob—"

Something large and dark suddenly appeared out of a narrow side road, engine roaring with ominous power. It struck their SUV side-on. As big as it was, the black SUV was lifted and pushed across the road, window glass shattering and showering the occupants. The passenger side of the SUV caved inward, metal buckling under the force created by the heavier vehicle that had rammed it.

The impact took them all off guard and tossed them around like rag dolls. Laura experienced a stunning blow to her body as she was forcibly slammed against the door. Her seat belt held for a moment then gave way and she felt herself being driven against the door frame. She heard sounds, voices, and then the heavy bark of gunfire.

Laura's hearing and sight were off-kilter; she couldn't make sense of anything. Her first instinct was to find out if her mother was all right. Nothing seemed to be working when she tried to locate her. Her limbs were loose and she couldn't sit up. Her head was full of raucous noise. She tasted blood in her mouth. Everything was a blur.

"Mom, can you hear me?"

The SUV creaked around her. Laura shook her head, blinked her eyes to attempt to clear them.

"Mom…"

She heard men calling to one another. There was anger.

The door she was slumped against was dragged open, metal protesting. Hands caught hold of her and she was dragged from the SUV, legs trailing across the door frame. Then she was outside, on the grass. She fought against the hands pinning her down, raging as much as she could against what was happening.

She could still hear the conflicted voices. They were arguing over something.

Laura tried to make it clear in her head, but she found herself fading, losing her hold on consciousness. She was grasped again by none-too-gentle hands and dragged across the ground. Then she lost her struggle and everything went dark…

"THE US MARSHALS vehicle was run off the road. Somebody used a stolen Kenworth tractor unit to ram it side-on and wrecked it…"

Bolan listened to Brognola's report as the big Fed went through what had happened. He waited until Brognola paused before he spoke.

"Casualties?"

"Marshal Trenton was shot to death. His partner, Carson, is in hospital. He was injured in the crash and also took a couple of bullets. I'm on my way there as we speak. The report I received said the doctors believe he'll pull through. The guy is young, fit and already fighting."

"What about Gwen and Laura?"

"They had to cut Gwen out of the vehicle. She was pinned in the wreckage. Early reports say she has a fractured thigh and hip. Ribs, as well. She lost a significant amount of blood."

"Laura?"

"We don't know if she was injured, Striker. All we do know is that she was taken from the scene by whoever engineered the crash."

"Taken?" Bolan said. "You mean she's been kidnapped."

"It looks that way."

The phone fell silent. Brognola didn't need to ask why. He could almost feel the Executioner's anger. Bolan was weighing the odds against Sherman walking out of the situation alive.

"Striker?"

"Yeah, I'm still here. Hal, do something for me."

"Name it."

"Is Carl Lyons available?"

Carl "Ironman" Lyons was the head of one of Stony Man's combat teams. Lyons had been an L.A. cop when he'd first come in contact with Bolan. Initially he'd been set on bringing the Executioner down. Eventually, Bolan's adversary had become a convert and aided the soldier on his quest for justice. When Stony Man was established, Lyons was brought in to form Able Team, along with Rosario Blancanales and Hermann Schwarz. They had quickly become a powerful and effective fighting team. Lyons, on his own, was a fearsome operative. He had a loathing for criminals and a reputation as a no-holds-barred fighter. It was in his nature to go all-out when it came to handling problems. Lyons was not the kind to show fear—and definitely no mercy to any opponent.

"He's on-site as we speak, in the armory with Kissinger working on his Python."

"This snatch had to be based on the mob getting information from an inside source. Someone in the Marshals department passed along details of the route Trenton and Carson were taking. Have Aaron get his team checking all sources. Run it down, Hal. Find the bastard who sold out. We need a name and then I want everyone to walk away. Let Carl have the sellout." Silence again. "The rule book goes out the window on this one, Hal. Get me a name and hand it to Ironman."

Brognola knew exactly what Bolan wanted.

This was going to be a job to be worked in Executioner mode.

No rules. No referee.

If he had feelings for the man who had sold out his badge, Brognola was about to push them in a dark corner and walk away.

"CRAIG DELVECCHIO," Akira Tokaido said. "He's a Des Moines resident with mob connections. He has no convictions, but he's danced on the edge. The local PD has him on their watch list. He's into IT. I'm downloading details now. I'll send the info along."

"So where does he fit into this?" Bolan asked.

He was on a conference phone connection with Tokaido, one of Kurtzman's cyber sleuths, along with Brognola and Lyons.

"I ran a background check on him," Tokaido said. "Delvecchio likes to figure he's a top-flight hacker. The guy does have skill, but he's not so smart when it comes to hiding his signature."

"Tell me he's been running searches on the Darrows."

"You got it. He ran a search through the Des Moines PD computer system using Darrow as a priority highlight. He came up with communication emails from the PD to the Des Moines Marshal facility. They asked for a Marshals Service escort to take the mom and daughter into protective custody. It was granted, and Des Moines PD was given a time for pickup."

"The mob simply had to work to that to plan their intercept," Bolan said.

"Looks that way," Lyons agreed.

"One marshal dead. Gwen Darrow and the other marshal in hospital. Laura a hostage."

Tokaido heard the hard tone in Bolan's voice as he made the statement.

"And Delvecchio gets a healthy bonus," Tokaido said. "I did some hacking and located an account he has in the Caribbean under his mother's maiden name."

"Not so healthy if we can do anything about it," Bolan replied. "Thanks for the help, Akira. You okay to handle this, Carl?"

"No sweat, Mack."

A ping told Lyons that data was being downloaded to his sat phone. He opened the message and studied the details of Delvecchio's driver's license. The photo showed a guy in his late thirties, with thick, pale blonde hair and a fixed stare on his broad face. A second message arrived with the satellite navigation details to his position.

"Leave this with me," Lyons said.

"Plane's warming up now," Brognola told him before they signed off.

Lyons pocketed his sat phone, grabbed his gear and headed for the exit, meeting Charlie Mott, Stony Man's standby pilot, at the front door of the farmhouse.

"Ready when you are."

"Let's go."

They crossed to the airstrip and climbed aboard a waiting chopper.

"Where are we headed?"

"All the way to Des Moines," Lyons replied.

He showed Mott the picture of the suspect.

"Is this our guy?"

"Yeah."

Mott tapped the flight coordinates into the helicopter's navigation system and powered up the helicopter.

"I take it we're not making a social call," Mott said.

"A call, yes. There's nothing social about it, in the true sense of the word."

"So you're not about to make someone's day?"

"Not in the way they'd want it," Lyons stated.

"There are days when you can be one enigmatic hombre."

"So true," Lyons said and settled back for the flight.

STREETLIGHTS WERE FLICKERING to life as Mott guided the SUV to the curb in front of the apartment building. He cut the engine and they sat studying the place.

"Third floor. On the corner."

"The lights are on," Mott noted.

Lyons checked his .357 Colt Python.

"Cover my six."

"Done."

They crossed the quiet street and entered the building. Lyons made for the stairs, Mott following. The floor was deserted. Lyons made his way along, counting off doors until he reached Delvecchio's apartment.

"Let's hope he doesn't have company," Mott said.

Lyons didn't answer as he stepped back, raised his right foot and slammed it into the door on a level with the lock. Every ounce of the Able Team leader's strength went into the kick. The door burst open and Lyons went in fast, Mott right behind him. The moment he cleared the frame Mott closed the door and stood with his back to it, holding it closed.

Lyons scanned the room as he went inside, searching and finding the guy he was looking for.

Craig Delvecchio had pushed himself up off the armchair, turning to cross the room and make for a door on the far side. He almost made it before Lyons caught up with him, clutching at the guy's loose shirt.

The blond ex-cop hauled the man to a stop, closing his fingers over the collar of the shirt. He swung Delvecchio around, spinning him off his feet and sending him crashing into a leather couch. The hardman gave a yell of alarm as he rolled over the couch, toppling it as he fell. He landed facedown on the carpeted floor, with barely enough time to register what was happening before Lyons stood over him, taking a handful of the man's hair and pulling him to his knees.

"Make this easy for me, Delvecchio. Don't cooperate so I can shoot you with a clear conscience."

Delvecchio felt the cold steel of the Python grind against his cheek.

"Jesus," he said. "What the fuck are you doing?"

"Making a point," Lyons growled. "Letting you know this isn't a fun visit." He stepped back and gestured for Delvecchio to get to his feet.

"Who the hell are you?" Delvecchio stared at Lyons and then looked over his shoulder at Mott lounging by the door. "You can't come in here pointing a gun—"

"Having the gun means I can do just about anything I want," Lyons said. "I'll make it easy. Answer the questions and we'll go."

"Questions? What questions?"

"Where was Laura Darrow taken?"

The flicker of unease in Delvecchio's eyes gave away his knowledge of the name. He tried to bluff it out, anyway.

"I don't know what you're talking about. Who the hell is she?"

Lyons lowered the Python and slammed his fist into Delvecchio's jaw. The force of the blow drove the guy's lips back against his teeth. Blood spattered from his mouth as he stumbled backward. He connected with a low, glass-topped coffee table and went down in a glittering explosion of glass, landing hard on his back.

Lyons stood over him, betraying nothing on his face.

"I don't like having to keep asking the same question," he grumbled.

Delvecchio moved sluggishly, spreading his arms as he tried to sit up. Shards of glass sliced at his hands. He held them up and stared at the bright blood wetting his hands.

"You passed data about the transport of Gwen Darrow and her daughter to your mob contacts," Lyons said evenly. "You told them the time and place so they could intercept. We've got it all, Delvecchio."

Lyons had filled Mott in with the information on the way to Des Moines.

"The payoff in your Caribbean account," Mott interjected. "It's a terrible thing using your mother's maiden name, Craig."

Lyons bent, took hold of Delvecchio and pulled the man upright. He swung the man around and slammed him against the wall with enough force to break the plaster and rattle Delvecchio's teeth.

"I still don't have my answer, Delvecchio. What did they do with Laura Darrow?"

"What if I don't know?"

"Then you're in worse trouble than you might imagine. You're down as accomplice to the death of a US Marshal. Another one is in the hospital alongside Gwen Darrow. Laura Darrow was kidnapped. That's a pretty damning list, Delvecchio."

"Brother, you'll be staring at four gray walls for years. Most likely the rest of your life," Mott added. "They do say those federal joints make hard time really hard."

"Are you trying to scare me?"

"I think he's succeeding," Lyons said. "I'd think about making a deal. This is a one-time offer. Personally, I don't give a damn. It's your choice. But I'd take a long, hard look at your situation."

Lyons glanced at Mott. The Stony Man pilot took out his sat phone and speed dialed the Farm.

"Delvecchio is ours," he said when Brognola answered. "No, he's in one piece. A little shaken up, is all... He's considering that, since we advised him of his possible chances... Deal? That will need to come from you in the light of any useful information he gives us."

Mott passed the phone to Lyons.

"I don't see any real chance of a deal for him," Brognola said. "He broke too many rules and a US Marshal is dead, another wounded. Gwen Darrow, as well. He's in deep."

"Might as well shoot him then," Lyons said. "Who the hell is going to care?"

"I'll leave that in your capable hands."

Lyons ended the call and passed the phone back to Mott. He made a play of checking his revolver.

"What the hell are you doing?"

"This? The decision has been made, Delvecchio. You screwed up and people are dead. So..."

Delvecchio looked from Lyons to Mott, who simply shrugged.

"Sorry, man. I just follow orders. They say terminate, I go along."

"What are you guys? Executioners?"

Lyons merely smirked.

Delvecchio held out for a few more seconds then held up his shaking hands.

"Back off," he said. "There's no need to do anything. What the hell... I'll give you what you need to know."

Lyons looked slightly disappointed, as if he preferred it when a perp made less of an effort.

"Make it the right information," he said, "because if I have to come back empty-handed, you will not like it."

# 14

"Do you ever get the feeling we're going around in circles?" Fresco asked.

He was sitting behind the wheel of the SUV he and Killian were in, heading for the location where Laura Darrow was being held. Their helicopter ride had put them down at the closest safe landing spot where they transferred to the waiting vehicle.

By the time they had touched down, the news concerning the strike had reached them. The US Marshals had been hit, but only Laura Darrow had been taken. Her mother had been trapped in the damaged transfer SUV, injured, and the snitch team had only been able to grab the younger woman.

Killian didn't speak. He was still less than happy at being dispatched to handle the interrogation of just the young woman instead of both. He didn't voice his thoughts when Danichev had called with the news.

Killian would do his seething quietly, and his partner, Fresco, understood the man's reticence. You didn't go around questioning people like Danichev. Not if you wanted to remain healthy. Too much had happened, was still happening, and from Bulova down there was a great deal of unrest within the organization.

The minute Harry Sherman had taken off, after copying Conte's files, sanity had gone out the window. It hadn't helped that Luca D'Allesandro had screwed up big-time by having a loose trigger finger. His wild shooting and failure to put Sherman down had thrown everything up in the air.

Finding Harry Sherman was the priority. Killian and Fresco had been handed that task and neither of them wanted it.

"Left to me, that Darrow bitch would have a bullet in the head already," Fresco said.

"Jake, it isn't what we want," Killian replied. It was the first thing he'd said for the past few miles. "Do you think I enjoy playing Danichev's game? I don't. Let's do the interrogation and get this over with.'

The voice of the satellite navigation system told Fresco they were approaching the area. He slowed the SUV, not wanting to overshoot. He saw the decaying bulk of the massive apartment building behind the wire fencing and rolled to a stop. He climbed out and opened the access gate so he could drive onto the site. One of the local hired shooters came out to meet them, dangling his subgun from one hand.

"Best to park around back," he said. "Out of sight."

His attitude didn't sit well with Killian. He held back from punching the guy in the mouth. The shooter stepped back as Fresco powered the SUV around the building and parked next to two other vehicles. As they climbed out, the shooter sauntered up to direct them to the entrance.

"You got a name?" Fresco asked.

"Jessup. Why?"

"I always like to know who I'm dealing with."

"You guys special or something?"

Killian managed a thin smile. "Or something."

"What's that mean?" Jessup asked.

"It means we'll remember you when we're done here," Killian said.

Jessup showed them the front entrance and then ambled off to continue his watch.

"Local talent," Fresco said. "Hicks with guns. That scares me."

There was another armed man standing inside the entrance.

"We've got people all around the place," the guy said.

Fresco smiled. "That makes me feel really safe."

"Where's the girl?" Killian asked and the man led them along the dusty passage and showed them a door.

Killian and Fresco entered the bare apartment and found a number of armed men inside.

"Is she that tough?" Fresco asked. "One girl?"

His attempt at humor got nothing but blank stares.

"Who's in charge?" Killian queried.

"Me. I'm Connolly. Are you Killian?"

That got him a sharp nod.

"Has she said anything?"

Connolly, a tall, lean-faced man, shook his head. "She's got a smart mouth but not the words we want to hear."

"Maybe you need to make her sing louder," Fresco said. "There's nobody around to hear."

"We were told not to make it so she couldn't," Connolly replied.

"Well, the big boys are here now, so let's see just how tough Miss Darrow really is," Killian said.

**15**

The housing project had ground to a halt at the halfway point because the money had run out, even though some of the ground-floor apartments had been near completion when the construction stopped. A chain-link fence surrounded the property, weeds growing up at its base. The sprawling block of the building was surrounded by abandoned machinery and piles of material.

"Why the hell would they bring her here?" Mott asked.

Lyons cut the engine and scanned the area. The site was surrounded by abandoned properties, the atmosphere desolate.

"Why not?" he said. "They want isolation. Somewhere no questions get asked and there are no nosy neighbors."

He had parked a distance from the project site, pulling the SUV into a shadowed space between a couple of abandoned houses.

Lyons contacted Stony Man for information about the site.

"The project is in construction limbo," Kurtzman told him. "The money ran out a couple of years ago. Since then no one has showed enough interest to start up again. The owners have just abandoned the place."

"Any security on the premises?"

"That was cut a few months back. The local PD makes the occasional sweep, but even they have minimal interest. Plenty of legitimate work to take up their time."

"Okay, Aaron. Thanks. I'll keep you updated."

Lyons glanced across at Mott. "Looks like it's just you and me, Charlie."

Mott smiled. "Not the first time," he said.

Lyons checked the sky. It was late afternoon and still bright. Distant clouds hinted at inclement weather.

"All set?" he asked.

Mott nodded. "Good to go."

The Farm pilot wore dark clothing and a much used leather jacket, zipped up over his 9 mm Beretta pistol.

Lyons was clad in black and carried his Python in a shoulder rig. He had a 9 mm Uzi on a shoulder strap and his Tanto combat knife in a sheath at his waist.

Each man carried a compact transceiver for communication if they got separated.

"The priority is getting Laura out unharmed," Lyons said. "Anyone in the way is treated as hostile."

"Let's hope she's here now that we've put in all this effort."

"Have faith," Lyons said. "We don't have much else going for us."

They exited the SUV and cut around the empty

houses as they approached the chain-link fence, using the overgrown foliage for cover. Crouched, Lyons pointed out the fresh tire-track impressions in the soft earth.

"Now you're doing your Tonto tracking thing," Mott said. "But I've got to agree that those imprints look new."

Lyons jabbed a finger at the metal-frame gates that allowed access to the site. The chain that hung in place had been loosened, the padlock open and dangling from one of the end links. He scanned the path leading across the site and glimpsed the tail end of a vehicle parked behind a corner of the building.

"Visitors," he said.

They both unholstered their handguns, Lyons leading the way as they eased in through the gates. Immediately they slid out of sight behind an untidy stack of concrete blocks, sundry weeds sprouting from the base. Concealed, they were able to fully assess the area.

"Should we expect sentries?" Mott asked.

"Always *expect*," Lyons said, "then you don't get caught off guard."

"Now you sound like one of those wise Chinese gurus."

"On your ten," Lyons said. "One guy. Just beyond that pile of rebar."

Mott picked up the movement and saw a figure dressed in dark pants and shirt, with a light sport coat. The guy had a hand resting on the butt of a pistol pushed behind his belt. Even from where Lyons and Mott crouched, they could see the bored expression on the sentry's face.

"He doesn't look as if he's in tune with the program," Mott said.

"Then we need to shake him up."

"I can do that."

Mott eased away from Lyons, using scattered piles of building materials for cover. By the time the Stony Man pilot moved in from the rear, the sentry was looking down at his shoes and scuffling restlessly in the dust.

The moment he was in position, Mott rose to his full height behind the man, striking without hesitation. His right arm curved around the guy's neck, left hand pressing the skull forward as Mott put on the pressure, cutting off his air. The strike was over quickly. Mott lowered the unconscious sentry to the ground, pulling him out of sight. He secured him with riot cuffs at wrists and ankles. With that done, he gave Lyons a signal and headed for the rear of the apartment building, leaving Lyons to handle the frontal approach.

LYONS MADE A FINAL weapons check. He unzipped one of his jacket pockets and took out a custom-made suppressor. John "Cowboy" Kissinger, the Farm's armorer, had adapted a Beretta 92-FS to take the screw-on accessory. Lyons attached the matte black tube, made sure it was settled and then wormed his way toward the front of the building, ducking below the level of dust-streaked windows. He slipped noiselessly inside through the doorless entrance. Settled dust on the concrete floor showed recent activity, providing Lyons with clear tracks, a number of footprints and a trail of drag marks.

Mott contacted him through his transceiver headset to advise there were a number of vehicles parked out of sight toward the rear of the building. More opposition, Lyons noted.

As he soft-footed inside, he saw someone moving ahead of him. The guy, armed, had his back to Lyons. Despite the Able Team commando's quiet tread, something had alerted the man and he spun around, pulling up the subgun he carried.

Lyons leveled the 92-FS and triggered a single shot, the suppressor lowering the sound of the shot to a low tone. The 9 mm slug slammed home between the gunner's eyes. His head rocked back, his expression freezing on his face as he toppled to the concrete floor. As Lyons stepped forward he heard the ring of the brass casing from the shot as it hit the floor. He checked the space around him, eyes and ears seeking anything that might tell him he had more company.

Nothing.

Ahead of him, on his right, he made out the cavernous opening of a pair of elevator shafts. The left wall exposed two temporarily placed plywood doors. The second door was where the footprints ceased.

Moving closer, Lyons picked up muffled sounds. Conversation.

One, a female voice raised in angry protest, sounded young. Lyons immediately picked up the inflection. It had to be Laura Darrow, resisting her captors.

As Lyons put away the Beretta and brought his familiar Colt Python into play, his transceiver clicked on.

"I'm in position," Mott stated. "There's another guy on guard back here."

"Could be others inside, so watch your six. I found our group. Second apartment on the ground floor. I'm going in. Come find me."

"You got it."

Lyons faced the plywood.

Raising a booted foot, he kicked the door open and rushed inside as it slammed back.

**16**

The Able Team leader's entrance caught the first pair of hardmen off balance. His Python snapped out a pair of .357 Magnum slugs that hit the duo before they could raise their subguns. The closest guy twisted away from Lyons, his chest punctured by the powerful round. He stumbled and slammed into the wall, his weapon slipping from his grasp. The man's partner took the next shot in his face, a chunk of bloodied flesh blown clear as he fell, his gun dropping from his grasp.

Jamming the revolver back into its holster, Lyons snatched up one of the dropped subguns and, still crouching, tracked in on the armed man who stood in the open arch that allowed access to the other section of the apartment. Lyons's finger stroked the trigger and sent a burning stream of slugs that chewed the guy's legs out from under him. The shooter hit the floor, squirming in agony. Lyons's second burst silenced him.

"Hold it there."

Lyons swung the subgun to cover the man who had

spoken. He recognized Anatole Killian from the photos the Farm had forwarded to his sat phone. The man stood close to Laura Darrow, one arm around her shoulders, the muzzle of his pistol pressed to the side of her head. She was staring directly at Lyons, face pale, eyes wide. The left side of her face was bruised and blood ran from the corner of her mouth, bright against her skin.

A second gunman stepped in front of Killian, his subgun partly raised.

"Move the gun away from me," Killian ordered Lyons.

The Able Team leader lowered the subgun.

"This is difficult," Killian stated.

"I thought this was a safe place," the other man complained.

"We guessed wrong, Fresco."

"Damn," Fresco said. "Just do the girl and let me off this bastard."

"Kill her and we lose our connection to Sherman."

"It's worth the risk."

The threat was not missed by Lyons. He glanced at Fresco. The man was primed to kill; it was there in his eyes. All he needed was the go-ahead from Killian.

"You want me to—?" Fresco asked.

"Don't be so eager, Jake," Killian chided. "I need to know what our friend here has to say."

"He shouldn't *say* anything."

"A man who is about to die has a right to speak."

Killian turned his eyes back to Lyons. "Just give Sherman up. That's all we want."

"You know it isn't going to happen," Lyons grumbled.

"Enough…" Fresco grit his teeth. "I'm going to cap

this son of a bitch right now. Then I can go back to work on the girl just like you want."

"Jake," Killian said to bring the guy back to the job at hand.

Fresco's head snapped around as he looked across at Killian.

Autofire sounded from the rear of the building. It was distant but unmistakable.

Charlie Mott was making his presence known.

The muzzle of Fresco's subgun moved fractionally as he registered the gunfire—and Lyons made his move, knowing this was the only chance he was going to get. His instinct told him Killian wouldn't kill Laura Darrow outright. She was his connection to Sherman, and he wasn't going to risk losing that. Fresco was the loose cannon, more likely to do something reckless.

Lyons dropped, hitting the floor on his right shoulder and executing a swift roll that kept him in motion and below the line of Fresco's weapon. He kept the subgun on line and, as he came out of the roll, angled the muzzle up at Fresco. The man's yell was drowned in the jarring rattle as the subgun fired, sending its burst at Fresco. It caught him just above the waist, the slugs carving their way into his body, angled upward so that they cleaved flesh and organs in a moment of destruction. Fresco fell back. Lyons heard his subgun fire, picking up a startled yell from Killian as a stray slug burned his right cheek.

Killian's grip loosened as he reacted to the burn and Lyons saw the girl shake herself clear. She had the presence of mind to fall to her knees, exposing Killian in the process.

Lyons fired, the burst hitting Killian in the face, channeling in through his skull and blowing out the back of his head. The former mob goon dropped without a sound.

Getting to his feet, Lyons moved to where Laura crouched. He slipped a big hand under her arm and pulled her to her feet.

"We have to get out of here," he said, hauling her toward the shattered door.

They cleared the doorway and turned toward the exit.

An armed man lunged into view, moving fast, his momentum driving him into Lyons. Briefly locked together, the pair struggled, Laura being pushed aside as they fought to gain the advantage. The gunman was strongly built under his expensive suit, but he'd met his match in the hard-bodied ex-cop. Neither man could clear his subgun, being so close to the other.

Lyons raised his right foot and slammed it down. He heard bone snap. The wounded gunman pulled away, struggling to stay upright, but his injury held him back. Lyons dropped to a crouch, pushing his weapon against the other man's torso.

In the second before his adversary fired, the guy realized his position and tried to react. Lyons pulled the trigger, sending a burst into the guy's lower body. The stream of slugs plowed in and through, severing the spinal cord. The man lost all control, his weightless mass slumping to the floor.

"Behind you!" Laura cried, her warning bringing Lyons around.

He spotted two shooters along the corridor toward the rear of the building. They were headed their way.

"Stay down," he growled.

Autofire rang out and the advancing shooters were driven to the floor as Charlie Mott appeared behind them. The Stony Man pilot hit the pair hard, his concentrated bursts giving them no chance to lay fire on Lyons and Laura.

Mott advanced, stepping by the downed men.

"That's a hell of an entrance," Lyons commented.

Mott glanced at Laura Darrow.

"I always like to make a show for the ladies."

"You managed that," Lyons said.

"This is becoming a habit, people having to rescue me," Laura said. She stood, her hand touching her bruised face. The corner of her mouth was still bleeding. "Tell me you know Cooper. It's just the way he would have done things." Then she sobered. "Is my mother all right?"

Lyons nodded. "Recovering in hospital. We'll get you to her."

"Is she badly hurt?"

"She was, but she's had treatment. Laura, she's going to be hospitalized for some time, but I heard she's going to make a full recovery."

"That bad? This is a nightmare. What the hell is happening?"

She glanced at the bodies on the floor, a look of revulsion on her face.

"Uncle Harry has some explaining to do. A hell of a lot of explaining."

"Let's get out of here," Lyons said. "The sooner we get you back to your mother the better I'm going to feel."

He reached out to take her arm.

"We were supposed to be safe the last time," Laura quipped.

"I guarantee it this time around. No risks. A federal protection detail," Lyons said. "No chance of being compromised."

"Tell me about the two marshals. I don't remember what happened to them."

"Trenton died at the scene. The other one, Carson, was wounded.

"He's in the same hospital as your mother," Lyons told her, leading the way out of the apartment building.

"Those marshals..." Laura muttered as they made their way across the debris-scattered lot. "They were protecting Mom and me and now one is dead. Jeez."

As they climbed into the SUV, Lyons noticed Laura had become quiet, arms hugging herself as she stared out the window. Mott, who had joined her in the rear of the vehicle, was talking quietly to her.

Lyons turned the vehicle around and headed for the road. Using his sat phone's wireless connection, he contacted the Farm. When Price answered he updated her on the situation.

"Is Laura okay?"

"She will be. We're on our way to the chopper. We'll take Laura to the hospital."

"Are you guys okay?"

"Yeah."

"Is there anything we can do?"

"Advise Hal of the need for total security. You understand?"

"On board."

"These people have been through enough. They'll need twenty-four-hour protection from now on."

"All set up. Laura and her mother will be under federal protection with a full team from now on."

"Okay." Lyons signed off.

"Aaron got a hit on Sherman's credit card," Tokaido told Bolan. "At that rail station. Kelly's Junction. It looks like he bought a ticket on a trip that terminates at the border."

"I'm on my way."

"There might be a result on that package you believe Sherman sent. It's not confirmed yet, but you'll get the word if and when it's located."

"Hold it a minute, Akira," Bolan said. "I think I might have spotted Sherman's Jeep."

Bolan rolled to a stop and checked out the deserted vehicle. He noted the damaged suspension then checked the registration slip on the sun visor. It confirmed the vehicle belonged to Ben Justin.

"The vehicle had a breakdown," Bolan advised the cyber whiz.

"Sherman probably hitched a ride to Kelly's Junction."

"There's only one way to find out," Bolan said.

17

Bolan crossed the rails and stepped up onto the platform. He felt his sat phone vibrate as he headed into the office to check the schedule. It was Grimaldi.

"I'm ready to join you when I get the call," he said.

"Stay tuned."

"You spotted our boy yet?"

"Still on the lookout," Bolan replied.

"Watch your six."

"And all the other numbers."

Bolan made his way over to the ticket counter. The clerk seemed only too willing to help a Justice agent when Bolan discreetly flashed the badge he carried, courtesy of Stony Man. He also recognized Harry Sherman as the man in the photo Bolan showed him on his phone.

"That guy…" the clerk said. "I couldn't help but notice him. He was kind of jumpy, you know? Kept checking his watch like he was worried he might miss his ride. Soon as the train pulled in he was on board."

The man leaned across the counter. "Is he some kind of criminal?"

Bolan shook his head. "Just someone we need to have a word with. All pretty routine."

"He didn't look like anyone desperate. Kind of like a nice guy. Quiet-looking, you know?"

"Thanks for your help."

"No problem. Nothing much happens around here, so a little something out the ordinary is welcome."

You'll never know, Bolan thought as he left the office for the platform.

The locomotive's whistle sounded. As Bolan stepped up to enter the car in front of him, he saw two figures detach from the shadows at the far end of the platform. They climbed aboard the last car. There was something about them that put Bolan on alert.

If he had spotted a couple of the opposition, it was possible there might already be others on board. If that was the case, they would all be on the hunt for Sherman—just as Bolan was. The difference was in the bottom line.

Bolan was there on a rescue mission.

The Conte crew would have a different agenda, one that would promise nothing but grief for the accountant.

The locomotive blasted out its harsh sound again. Bolan felt the car vibrate as the train jerked into motion. It picked up speed as it eased away from the station, pushing clear and heading north. Bolan slid his hand inside the leather jacket, feeling the textured grips of the 93-R. He had a full 20-round magazine in the pistol and two extra in the leather holder on his opposite shoulder. That and a razor-sharp lock knife were the only weapons in his arsenal. He had left his full complement of weapons with Grimaldi, so what he was carrying was going to be his limit.

His priority was to locate Harry Sherman and convince him that he was one of the good guys. The soldier hoped the man would fall in with anything he offered. Sherman was going to be decidedly nervous. Bolan could relate to that. From the moment he'd stepped away from Conte and the mob, Sherman had become a moving target. He would remain as such as long as the team of shooters stayed on his tail. Bolan had no idea what the intention was—to take Sherman alive or to terminate him. Whichever, Sherman was going to find himself caught in a trap unless Bolan could keep him close.

He stepped into the car. He was going to have to check each one, searching for Sherman and keeping an eye out for the opposition, who would be doing the same.

There were two cars ahead of Bolan and three behind. He eased along the aisle, checking the seated passengers. The car he was in had no more than six occupants. None of them was Harry Sherman. Bolan kept moving, through into the next gently swaying car.

He slid the zip of his jacket down to allow himself easy access to his Beretta if he needed it. He was hoping it wouldn't be necessary to draw his weapon. Gunfire inside the restricted area of a rail car was not something Bolan wanted. He also realized he might not have a choice. Conte's men might not be concerned with such niceties. It was the difference between them. They didn't care much about collateral damage. Bolan did, and that could place him in a difficult position. Involving innocent civilians was not on Bolan's agenda. He would willingly place his own life on the line to keep others safe. The opposition had no such worry.

Bolan felt the car sway as the train eased through a wide curve. He braced himself as he continued his deliberate trek along the aisle, reaching the end of the car without identifying Harry Sherman. That left one more car ahead before he would need to retrace his steps to check the cars behind him.

Easing through the connecting doors, Bolan entered the final car.

There were more passengers in this one. Bolan counted at least a dozen heads.

And Harry Sherman was one of them.

The accountant was seated alone and facing in Bolan's direction. He was recognizable from the image Stony Man had provided, though the expression on his face showed a different man from the photograph. The strain he was under had drawn dark lines under Sherman's eyes and it looked as if he had lost a few pounds. The way he was hunched in his seat told Bolan of the pressure the guy was under.

That was no surprise to Bolan. Since the moment of the shooting, when Conte's man had tried and failed to eliminate Sherman, the man had been on a constant run for his life. The strain was showing.

Bolan moved along the car. He adopted a casual stance, not wanting to alarm Sherman. In the man's present state of mind, it wouldn't take much to panic him. Even as he approached the accountant's seat, Bolan could see the suspicion in Sherman's expression. His body had tensed up, and it appeared that the guy was ready to leap to his feet and take off.

Coming level with Sherman's position, Bolan sat in

the facing seat, both hands in plain sight. He saw Sherman pull back, pressing against the seat, color rising in his cheeks.

"Easy, Harry," Bolan said. "I'm a friend of Leo's. He asked me to help. Right now I'm all you've got."

Sherman made no concession to relaxing. His whole attitude was tense, his eyes flicking back and forth, a man seeking a way out, an escape, and knowing there was little he could do to achieve that.

Bolan kept his voice low, his tone level.

"I know what you're up against, Harry. That Conte is searching for you. He's already made moves against your family."

"*What?* Are they okay?"

"They were in a car crash when Conte tried to have them snatched from US Marshals. Gwen was hurt and Laura kidnapped. Your sister is in hospital. My people took Laura away from the kidnappers, and they're both in protective custody now. Harry, they're safe. But you're not. That's why I'm here. To make sure you stay clear of Conte's people."

"You have backup?"

"No, there's just me. I work alone." Bolan made a quick show of his Justice credentials.

"What do I call you?"

"Cooper. Now listen to me, Harry. We have company on this train. I already spotted two and there might be others."

"How did they find me?"

"We're talking about the mob. They have ways. Right now that isn't important. We need to concentrate on dealing with the situation we're in."

"Did they get to Ben? He helped me."

"They got to him. He's hurt but alive."

"It looks like I'm making a lot of trouble for people, Cooper. All because Conte decided I tried to steal from him and put me on the spot." Sherman shook his head. "This has to end. Cooper, I found computer files that will put Conte and his whole organization in jail. I found the information by accident, but right now it's my only way out of this. We have to get hold of it."

"Leo told his superiors about that. You don't have it with you?"

"No. I sent it to a safe place."

"Which is why you want to reach Canada?"

"Yeah. I was hoping I could shake Conte's people and get my hands on it."

"Then that's what we need to do, Harry."

"It's as easy as that?"

"I don't think so, but we'll try. I want you to do what I tell you, when I tell you. No questions. Understand me? Conte's men are not here to keep you healthy. Remember that."

"I figured I could get away. Take this train and lose myself." Sherman shook his head, seemingly resigned to whatever might happen to him. "I've been kidding myself. Conte isn't going to let me go. He'll follow me to hell and back."

"No, we're not going to let him do that. Look at me. I don't run with the losing team. Conte isn't going to come out on top. We won't let him."

"So what do we do?"

"We make our way to the rear, through each car, until we can't go any farther and see if we attract interest."

"Make targets of ourselves?"

"It's called being proactive, Harry. Let's see if we can draw Conte's men out into the open."

"You mean *moving* targets?"

Bolan stood. "Let's go. It's time to shake the tree."

"Great," Sherman said. "Hell, I never expected to live forever. Just a little longer than the end of the day."

Bolan looked over Sherman's shoulder and saw a tall figure moving forward from the far end of the car. The guy had a look on his face that told Bolan he wasn't looking for the toilet. The guy had his right hand under his coat and when he fixed his gaze on Bolan, the silent signal was obvious. He stopped short of Sherman's seat.

"This goes one of two ways,' he said. "The easy one is for you two walk to the far end of the car and through the door. Right through to the rear of the train. That, or I make a lot of noise and people around us start getting hurt. I'm guessing you don't want that to happen. Now, me? I wouldn't lose any sleep if that did happen."

The guy had read Bolan right. There was no way he was about to create a situation where other passengers might get hurt. Bolan kept his hands in sight, lowered to show he was staying calm.

"Just walk ahead," the guy said. "We can handle this with no fuss."

Bolan could see through the window of the connecting door to the last car. Beyond that was the baggage car.

"Hey, don't make this a day trip."

Impatience made him move up close and place his free hand against Bolan's spine, which became the Executioner's moment to react. As he felt the hand press against him, Bolan spun on the soles of his shoes, letting his arms follow the action of his body. He had turned to the right, and his left hand dropped to close over the gunman's right hand where it was concealed by the folds of his coat. Bolan levered down, preventing the guy from pulling his weapon. In the same moment the Executioner's right, edge on, slammed into the guy's neck. The blow was delivered with every ounce of his strength, the force behind it crunching in below the jawline.

Suddenly the guy found himself unable to breathe. He stepped back, his eyes wide with shock as he struggled, and failed, to suck in air. Somewhere down the car a man protested—he was ignored as Bolan hauled the gun hand into view. He snatched the pistol from his adversary's hand. It took no effort. The hood was too concerned with trying to breathe to offer any resistance.

"Cooper," Sherman said.

He pushed Bolan to the side a second before the window of the connecting door shattered. The window was glass, and splintered shards flew everywhere. The slugs meant for Bolan and Sherman slammed into the helpless hood, pushing him back. Someone yelled in panic. Passengers scrambled from their seats, crowding one another as they pushed through the connecting door at the opposite end of the car.

Bolan had his Beretta in his hand now. He tossed the pistol he'd taken from the hood to Sherman.

"If you need to shoot, just point and pull the trigger."

There was movement from the far car. Autofire crackled and slugs hammered the connecting door. The final shard of glass dropped from the frame.

"This is crazy," Sherman said. "They know we can't go anywhere, Cooper. I should have listened to my old man when he said I should have become a priest."

His words were ignored as Bolan assessed their position. In the confines of the rail car, there was no chance they could conceal themselves. They were in the open, with armed men facing them. Once the shooters decided to push their way through, it would become a turkey shoot. If Bolan had been on his own, he might have considered resisting. But he had Sherman to consider, plus the burden of the other passengers. If he put up a fight, any retaliatory gunfire could overlap and cause injury to the innocent. That was something Bolan refused to allow. The passengers were being drawn into a threatening scenario that had nothing to do with them. Mack Bolan would not consider that a viable risk.

He and Sherman were in line for the hostile fire. Bolan accepted that—with reservations where Sherman was concerned. The man was making an attempt to right wrongs, and he didn't deserve to become a victim himself.

The only way out was for Bolan and Sherman to remove themselves from the situation, which was easier to consider than to achieve. The soldier glanced at the window. The landscape slid by, an area of undulating terrain, wide and empty.

Another burst of autofire drove shots against the connecting door. This time a couple of slugs broke through.

Bolan had already considered what he knew to be his and Sherman's only option. He took that option and made his decision.

He triggered a triburst through the connecting door to force the opposition back, even if it was only a brief distraction.

"Harry, let's go," he said. "Stay low and head for the other door."

"What…?"

"Do it, Harry, before those guys come our way."

Bolan fired off another triburst.

Crouching, they made for the connecting door at the far end of the car. Bolan flung it open and hustled Sherman through. They paused on the swaying, open platform between the two cars, the rattle and rumble of the train loud in their ears.

The ground swept by, a spread of green below the slope that bordered the track.

Bolan glanced back through the connecting door and saw armed men moving into view. This time he held the Beretta in both hands and fired. Glass shattered. Bolan saw one man fall and the others pull aside. The delay would only last for seconds. He holstered the 93-R and zipped up his jacket.

"Have you ever jumped from a moving train?"

Sherman stared at Bolan. "Hell, no," he said.

"There's a first time for everything. Just let yourself go limp," Bolan said. "Tuck and roll."

Realization dawned as Sherman stared at him. Bolan didn't give him time to take in any more. He grasped Sherman's shoulders and pushed him from the rail car. Sherman fell out of sight, his startled yell whipped away as he tumbled into empty space.

Without another thought Bolan followed, feeling the air pull at him as he dropped. The green slope came up at him faster than he had expected and, as he attempted to follow the advice he had given Sherman, Bolan hit the ground. He twisted, spun, his breath driven from his body by the jarring impact. The sheer force of his landing left Bolan unable to control his momentum.

He went down the slope, turning over and over until he came to a sudden stop.

He lay facedown, making no attempt to move. It took him a few attempts before he was even able to drag air into his burning lungs and even then he lay still. When he finally did move, it was to check his arms and legs for any damage. Apart from aching muscles and bruised flesh, they felt okay. He had survived. He took his time standing, rubbing the side of his face where he had scraped it across the ground.

Bolan began to search for Sherman. He heard the man before he saw him. It seemed the man possessed a colorful vocabulary and was using every word he knew.

Sherman was on his knees when Bolan finally spotted him some yards away, his hands moving over his body as he checked himself out.

"I can't believe we just did that," Sherman said.

Bolan didn't answer. He simply caught hold of the man's coat and hustled him farther away from the tracks.

"We could have been killed." Sherman slapped at the dust clinging to his clothes. "Or ended up with broken bones."

"You prefer being shot?"

"What?"

"It was a simple question, Harry. Should we have stayed on the train and let those men shoot us?"

"Look, Cooper, it was a…"

"It was a simple choice, Harry. If we had stayed, we would have ended up dead. Instead we jumped and we're still alive."

Sherman touched his jawline where he had grazed it during the fall.

"Put like that, I guess not," he said.

"Let's go. It might seem that we're in the clear, but those guys on the train will be reporting what happened. Any time that we've gained needs to be used well."

"Meaning they'll still be looking for us?"

"Count on it."

Sherman shook his head. "So it's going to be a show-down here in the middle of nowhere? Cooper, maybe I'm not ready for a replay of *High Noon*. I never shot a gun in my life."

"But you can still run."

"Yeah? Not from the speed of a bullet from a gun."

"I'll try to keep that from happening."

Bolan took out his sat phone and speed-dialed Aaron Kurtzman.

"What have you got yourself into this time?" Kurtz-man said.

"We took a train then jumped off the train. Right now I could do with an assist to fix our position."

Kurtzman could be heard giving out instructions to his team. He was back on the line after a few minutes, updating Bolan on his position.

"Satellite GPS has you pinpointed. You need to keep moving north. You're about twenty miles from the near-est town and seventy from the border with Canada. The closest main road is nine miles from your current po-sition. Northeast. Get to that and it will take you to the town of Bishop, which is also the point where the rail tracks bisect the town."

"Very concise," Bolan said.

"I'm sending the coordinates to your phone."

"Thanks. Got it."

"I realize you're not exactly in the most favorable situation out there. We still have Jack in the wings. He could put that eggbeater in the air and be with you pretty quickly. Why walk when you can make the trip in style?"

"That was my next request. Forward him the coordinates and send him on his way. Just let him know we could have hostiles converging on our position. Leaving that train was a necessity. Our less-than-friendly followers won't have given up on us and they'll have backup, so the badlands here could be set to become even worse."

"You have this knack of moving from one bad situation to another with such consummate ease, Striker. How do you manage it?"

"I took a correspondence course in action management."

"Give them a call and request a refund. Brother, it's not working. Okay, details sent to Jack. He'll make contact and head for your location."

Bolan acknowledged and ended the call.

"Did I hear you say we could have visitors?" Sherman queried.

Bolan glanced up from checking the 93-R; he had eight left in the magazine and two extra magazines. He would have liked more but life didn't run on wishes.

"There's a pickup on its way, Harry. All we need to do is stay in the clear until my guy shows up."

"Let's hope Conte's men see it that way and leave us in peace."

Bolan checked their position, motioning to Sherman that they needed to move. They were on mostly open ground, with the rail track curving away from them, the train having vanished from sight.

"Let's go."

**18**

"Am I employing imbeciles?" Bulova snapped into the phone. "Was I expecting too much when I asked these morons to find Sherman? Did I not pay enough? Vitaly, tell me what is going wrong."

Danichev quickly drained the tumbler, clutching the phone to his ear as his mind raced to conjure up an answer that would satisfy his boss.

"They outflanked us," he said. "Passengers on the train heard Sherman call some guy who's helping him Cooper. This guy is no amateur. He must have military training."

"Should we give him a medal then? What am I hearing, Vitaly? It sounds like an excuse. From you, Vitaly?"

"We messed up—*I* messed up. No excuse, Serge. But we are not walking away. There are more men on the way now that Sherman and Cooper have left the train. They are on their own. We will find them."

"Let us hope so, Vitaly, otherwise we may all be on the fucking run. Do you understand me?"

"Yes, Serge."

The phone went silent. Danichev stared at it.

Things were not going as planned. Harry Sherman should have been in their hands by now. He should be dead. Or at least suffering and telling them all they needed to know. But that was not happening. Sherman was running free, accompanied a man named Cooper. He was the one who was keeping Sherman out of trouble and taking down every hired gun Danichev threw in his path.

Danichev wanted to know who the man was.

Where he came from.

He was no ordinary cop, not the way he acted. There was no denying the man was skilled. Deadly. And from the score he was ratcheting up Cooper had no concerns when it came to facing off against his adversaries. The man was a skilled operative. In most ways he was a step above the men Danichev had in the field.

Danichev tapped a number into his cell phone, waiting impatiently until it connected.

"Danson, we need this matter resolved. I just spoke with Bulova. He is not taking this well. And if he is unhappy, I am unhappy. This man, Cooper, is making us all look bad. Put everything we have into finding him and Sherman. I don't give a damn how much it costs, or how many people you have to bring in. Just find them, Danson. For God's sake find them and make Sherman deliver those files."

Danichev didn't wait for an answer. He ended the call and slammed the cell phone on the desk.

"I need a drink," he said. "A large one."

OSCAR DANSON, THE MAN on the spot, put away his phone and signaled his driver.

"Let's move," he said. "Forget the train. They can sort themselves out when it reaches the station. They'll have to catch a cab home. We need to turn around and go back. Pick up where Sherman and that guy, Cooper, jumped ship."

There were three SUVs. They had been tracking the train, waiting until it made a stop. The plan had been for the men on board to get to Sherman and hold him until the pickup could be made. Things had changed since the man Cooper had also got himself on board. The *easy* pickup had turned sour. Men were dead. Others wounded. And Danson had picked up a call from the train admitting that Sherman and Cooper had bailed, which meant they were on foot, somewhere back along the track. And the boss was pissed.

Danson stood with his team as they took in what he had to say.

"Who the fuck is this son of a bitch?" someone asked.

"Whoever he is, he's smart."

"You think? Maybe we should offer him a job when we find him," Danson said.

"Say what you like. He got Sherman off the train and left our boys holding their dicks," Frank Jellico replied.

Danson couldn't deny that.

"If we want ours to stay attached, we better catch up with Sherman. So let's get moving and bring this circus to an end."

The teams moved to the waiting vehicles and climbed in, the drivers turning and picking up speed as they ran parallel with the rail tracks. Weapons were checked and held ready. Whatever the end result, the confrontation was going to be bloody.

The terrain was uneven and despite the top-line suspension, the ride was uncomfortable.

"Where are those assholes?" Jellico asked. "There's nowhere out here to hide."

"Are you that eager to get yourself shot?"

"This Cooper isn't Superman," Alvin Palmer said.

"Yeah? Well, he handled the snatch team on his own," Danson stated. "You have respect for somebody like that."

"I'll tell you what I respect. The dollar bills I get paid for this work. Everything else is just crap."

"That's a sad thing to admit," Jellico claimed.

"He's a sad person," Danson said. "You know, I can't recall the last time I saw him smile."

"You guys want to concentrate," the driver said. "I think our targets are up ahead."

Danson peered out through the windshield and spotted two men coming into range fast.

"Palmer, here's where you get to earn those Franklins you love so much," Danson said. He slapped the driver on the shoulder. "Let's go get 'em..."

**19**

"There's no easy way to say this, Harry. Conte wants you dead and buried. There isn't going to be any kind of negotiating with him. No buying our way out. No last-minute changes of heart. You understand that?"

Sherman gave a half smile. "Gee, don't sugarcoat it, Cooper. Wrapping it in ribbon isn't any help. Yes, I get it. That man wants my head on a silver plate, delivered to his office so he can poke me in the eye and say I told you so. Cooper, I get the message. I got it on the train.

"Tell you what, though. I don't figure to let it happen. I'm not the one who did anything wrong. Not enough to get a kill order hung around my neck. I took my eye off the ball and some sleazebag stole a chunk of money I was supposed to be looking after.

"Damn it, Cooper, that's how all this started. Next thing I'm being put in the frame for that nine million. Now…that asshole Conte? The son of a bitch wants my life. He had to make a big deal out of it. You know one of the crazy things about this? Nine million is small change to the organization. People don't realize the money the mob makes every day. Those files took my blinders off. Suddenly Conte gets all righteous and I take the fall. But I've got that flash drive. Tough. We've all got trouble. Conte can go to hell. No way I'm being backed into a corner so his hired goons can shoot me."

"Tell me about the information, Harry."

"Conte kept details of every crooked deal he's ever made. Names. Dates. Amounts. He likes to make out he's a savvy guy, but underneath it all he doesn't trust anyone. He built this store of information, which is handy stuff to have in your hand if things go wrong. Cooper, those lists can point the finger at so many people you wouldn't believe it unless you saw it."

"And you won't tell me where the flash drive is until we're on safe ground?"

"Do you blame me?"

"No, I don't blame you. You've got yourself in a deep hole and it's falling in around you. All you want is to reach solid ground."

"Damn right. Look, Cooper, I'm not pleading innocence. I knew what was going on back there. I'm not such an idiot I didn't know who I was working for. Conte is a bad son of a bitch. Okay, I took his money every payday. So if that makes me as bad as him, what the hell can I say? I'll tell you this, and you either believe me, or not. I was an accountant, period. I was never involved in Conte's behind-the-door business. I knew he was involved in all sorts of shady stuff, but until this business with Lemke, I just kept my head down and my ears shut.

"The day Conte showed what he could do to me, the game was over. All the glitter and the drinks and the girls? That was the icing on a cake full of maggots. Behind the closed doors it was a nightmare, and I was part of it. One way or another, all those years, I'd let it go over my head. Pretended it wasn't anything to do with me. I just counted up the money, paid Conte's bills. Jesus, Cooper, I was fooling myself big-time. I was wallowing in the slime and it stuck to me."

Sherman was struggling for breath after his speech. His head rolled to one side and he stared at Bolan. "That's the longest speech I ever made in my life. I'm not trying to justify what I was involved in. I can't. And I guess what I'm doing is trying to talk my way out of that hole you mentioned... How am I doing so far?"

"We'll never get to be lifelong buddies, but I'll give you an A for effort. Right now that isn't our main concern."

Sherman was about to agree but sensed the man wasn't paying any more attention. He saw that Cooper had halted and was staring back along the way they had come.

Bolan had picked up faint sounds. He filtered out extraneous noise and focused on the overwhelming hum that could only mean one thing.

Powerful engines. More than one. Heading in their direction. Very fast.

He raised the Beretta, his finger resting against the trigger guard.

Sherman saw the move.

"Are you going to shoot something for lunch?" he asked. "Because if you are, it's going to be hard to start a fire."

"I wish it was as simple as that."

"Then what?"

A pair of matching SUVs came into view, speeding like metal dinosaurs over the curve in the terrain, wheels throwing up chunks of earth and spirals of dust. They gave the appearance of guided missiles as they slid around to target the two men.

"Cooper, this isn't looking too good."

Bolan had already scanned the immediate area. The only cover available was a hut belonging to the rail company, close to the tracks. It wasn't what Bolan would have chosen given anything else, but right then it was the only possible alternative to standing in the open.

"Harry, get in the hut. Just do it. *Now*."

Sherman broke into a run, pushing himself to the limit and knowing his best was far from extreme. He clutched the pistol in his hand, more for comfort than anything else. Behind him he could hear the increasing roar of the SUVs as they sped closer. As much as he wanted to, he refrained from turning to see what Cooper was doing. He just kept running and wondering why the hut didn't seem to be getting any closer...

BOLAN SET THE Beretta to single shot.

He faced a pair of targets that were growing larger with every passing second and needed to gain the maximum from his weapon. He wanted the vehicles within range to give him the best shot he could hope for. The SUVs were moving over rough terrain, bouncing on their suspensions, which only added to Bolan's problem. He was going to need to make calculated shots, his intention to target the drivers. The closer the vehicles came to where he was positioned, the better chance he stood.

The passenger window on the left vehicle powered

down and a figure leaned out, wielding a subgun. The muzzle angled in Bolan's direction and the guy opened fire. It was plain to see that he was having the same problem facing Bolan. The subgun jerked despite the shooter attempting to hold it steady. The stream of 9 mm slugs cleared the Executioner by yards.

Bolan tracked in on the guy, compensated for the rocky ride and triggered his first shot.

A miss.

The shooter responded with a second burst.

Well clear.

Bolan held his ground and moved his pistol to match the SUV's roll. He stroked the trigger, feeling the Beretta recoil.

The shooter jerked back, the 9 mm Parabellum round coring into his right shoulder and splintering the bone. The subgun slipped from his grip.

The second he had triggered his shot, Bolan brought the Beretta to the right, locking on the windshield. He fired once, then a second time. Behind the glass that suddenly splintered, the driver lost control, falling back from the wheel. With a suddenness even Bolan had not anticipated, the big SUV lurched sideways and slammed into the other vehicle. The scrape of clashing metal rose above the roar of the engines. Both SUVs slowed and came to jerking stops.

Bolan skirted the second vehicle. There was movement inside. A rear door was kicked open and an armed man tumbled out. He had a bleeding gash on his right cheek. As his feet hit the ground, he twisted, saw Bolan and raised his subgun. The Beretta flamed briefly as the Executioner put a single slug into the guy's chest, kicking him back. He slithered along the side of the SUV before dropping to the ground.

The crackle of autofire alerted Bolan to the fact that one of the passengers from the first SUV had started to fire his own weapon. He was out of the vehicle, moving around to clear the bulk of the car, firing wildly to cover himself. Bolan tracked him and fired twice. He saw blood spurt from the guy's throat as he stumbled and fell.

Movement to Bolan's left caught his attention and he dropped to a crouch, swinging the Beretta around. Another shooter from the first vehicle leaned against the SUV then stretched across the hood, bracing his subgun. The weapon flared with fire as he triggered a wild burst in Bolan's direction. The volley passed close enough for the soldier to feel a tug at his sleeve in the instant before he returned fire, triggering three fast, single shots that slammed into the shooter's head.

Before the guy hit the ground, Bolan dropped the partially empty magazine and clicked in one of his reserves, his experienced fingers completing the reload in seconds. With the Beretta fully loaded and now set for 3-round bursts, Bolan moved forward and snap-aimed at one of the attackers as he pushed his way from the second SUV. The guy arched back as a trio of 9 mm slugs punched into his upper chest. He toppled backward, triggering his subgun as he fell.

Bolan wasn't fully sure what triggered the sudden burst of flame from the rear of one of the SUVs. Maybe a fuel tank fractured when the two vehicles collided and something had generated the flash point; maybe an electric cable shorted out from the impact. The result was a spurt of fire. It coiled up from the close-standing cars, traveling their length and reaching up to the roofline. The volatile mix of vapor and oxygen combined to increase the volume and after a few seconds of what seemed like hesitation, the savage blast of exploding gasoline threw a shock wave that reached Bolan. He felt the push of the concussion and the heat that followed it. The SUVs were engulfed as the writhing ball of flame blossomed. It roared its energy, ripped at the bodywork of the vehicles and shattered glass. Any gunners still inside the SUVs were caught in the encompassing inferno.

Bolan pulled back. The gunfight was over. He turned and made for the hut where Sherman had taken cover. The man was standing just inside the weathered timber door, his face drained of color.

A second gasoline explosion blew a ball of flame skyward, leaving the pair of SUVs blazing wrecks.

"Cooper, this is getting way out of hand. What the hell is Conte's game?"

"It's called covering all bases. These people don't quit and walk away if they're threatened. Whatever is in the data you found, it's capable of bringing down their house. They're going to pull out all the stops to prevent that."

Bolan turned at a sound coming from behind them.

A third SUV was heading their way from the opposite direction.

The passenger window was down and a gunman holding a subgun was hanging halfway out. He loosed a long burst that splintered the hut's sides.

Bolan stepped back, slamming Sherman into the open doorway and ducking low as the SUV swept in close, the shooter opening fire again. The slugs blew holes in the wall a few feet from where Bolan crouched.

As the vehicle rolled by, the Executioner triggered the Beretta, firing a trio of 9 mm Parabellum rounds that caught the shooter in the chest. The gunner uttered a strangled cry as the slugs ripped into his torso, snapping bone and fatally tearing through organs. He slumped over the door frame, the subgun dropping from his grip. It came to rest a few yards from the hut. Bolan jammed the Beretta back into the shoulder holster, cleared the hut and snatched up the weapon, making a rapid check. With the acquired weapon in his possession, Bolan pulled back inside the hut, watching as the SUV circled and came to rest a dozen yards away.

He saw three men scramble from the vehicle, all armed. They took up positions behind the bulk of the SUV and turned their weapons on the hut.

"Stay down," Bolan said. "Low as you can get."

One of the men behind the SUV fired a burst. The grime-encrusted window Bolan was close to burst in a shower of glass. He felt fragments hit his clothing. One sliver scored his cheek, slicing the flesh; blood streaked his face. He pulled the subgun around and returned fire, seeing the shooters react as his slugs punched holes in the SUV.

Another of the SUV's crew made a run at the hut, firing as he came. Leaning around the door frame, Bolan tracked the moving target, held, then fired. The burst took the guy in the side, spinning him and dropping him to the ground.

From where he was crouched, Bolan had a clear view of the SUV. Two more shooters were waiting for their chance.

The Executioner checked the landscape. Nothing

save for the black smoke rising from the original two vehicles.

The surviving shooters were biding their time.

It was possible that one of them was on his cell phone calling for backup. The thought didn't settle well with Bolan. The last thing he needed right now was more guns showing up; he had a limited amount of ammunition. What he had wasn't going to last forever...

Bolan picked up a distant but familiar sound, faint, but growing in volume.

The sound of rotors beating the air.

Helicopter.

Bolan hoped it was the one Grimaldi was piloting.

He slipped his phone from his pocket and sat-linked to Grimaldi's comm unit. It pinged a couple of beats before the recognizable voice came through.

"That bonfire for me?" Grimaldi asked.

"It's that kind of neighborhood."

"It always is when you show up, Sarge. Hey, are you clear?"

"Uh-uh. I've got two hostiles close by."

"ETA is two minutes. Pity I don't have any ordnance on board."

"You on the way is all I'll need. Out."

Bolan dropped the sat phone back into his pocket. He double-checked the borrowed subgun.

"Are we okay?" Sherman asked.

"Getting there."

Bolan scanned the SUV. He could see booted feet moving the length of the vehicle. The opposition was on the move.

He had no idea what they were planning and didn't feel inclined to wait to find out.

Bolan flattened on the hut floor, extending the sub-gun out the door and targeting the underside of the SUV, tracking the men's movement. His finger rested lightly against the trigger as he waited for his opportunity. It came when one guy paused just short of the rear wheel.

Bolan eased the trigger back and rode the subgun's recoil as it fired off a long burst. The wheelbase of the SUV was high enough to expose the half-calf length of one guy's legs. The slugs ripped into his limbs. The guy whipped around under the solid impact, his legs shattered and torn. He went down hard and Bolan could hear his screams of pain as he flailed on the ground.

The surviving hood made a wide circle around to the front of the SUV, coming into view as Bolan pushed to his feet and ran forward, pounding his way across the rough ground.

He met the shooter face to face, each man raising his weapon. The hardman took a second to assess the situation then fired off a long burst. His shots were off the mark; Bolan's were not. He tracked in with his subgun and fired off a burst that ripped into the target's center mass. The guy arched under the impact, his arms flailing, and went down on his back, a spray of blood bursting from his mouth.

Bolan rounded the back end of the SUV, tracking the subgun ahead. The man he had shot in the legs was down but not out, despite the agony of his wounds. A subgun was on the ground close by. The gunman had a pistol in one bloody hand, and he thrust it in Bolan's direction when the Executioner eased into view. The pistol cracked sharply, the slug clanging against the body of the SUV.

He thrust the pistol in Bolan's direction a second time, his finger hard against the trigger.

Bolan swept the subgun around, the long burst chewing at the ground as the soldier walked the volley into his adversary's torso, hammering unforgiving slugs into his flesh, stopping the shooter.

After quickly checking the bodies and distancing the weapons, Bolan took the sat phone from his pocket and reconnected with Grimaldi.

"It's safe to come in, Jack," he said. "I've plowed the road for an easy landing. Come and get us out of here."

Bolan turned to give the all-clear to Sherman and saw the man facedown in the doorway of the hut.

He ran toward Sherman, but before he reached him he knew there was nothing he could do. Sherman's skull was a shattered mess of bone, blood and brains that leaked onto the ground.

Bolan stared down at the still form. It was not the end he had been expecting for Harry Sherman. Not after everything that had happened to the man and his family.

Gwen and Laura would need to be told. So would Leo Turrin. They had all been involved from the start. It would be something Bolan would take on. Something he needed to do.

He was still standing there when Grimaldi walked up from the helicopter.

"Hell, Sarge, I'm sorry. The poor guy was only trying to do the right thing."

Bolan looked up, his eyes bleak but starting to show the anger inside.

"And that's what we need to do, Jack…the right thing."

**20**

It was midafternoon when Mack Bolan entered the casino from the hot glare of the Vegas street. He made his way through the crowd, a determined man with only one thing on his mind.

Cutting across the casino floor, he cleared the gaming tables and banks of slot machines, ignoring the noise and the glittering lights. The rear section of the establishment was closed off by a set of double doors. Bolan shouldered them open, walking through as they swung back into place behind him. The din of the main casino was cut off by the soundproofing. The reserved section containing store rooms and offices had a cathedral hush after the clamor. Even the lighting was low-key.

Bolan wore civilian dress: dark slacks and a light jacket. Under the jacket Bolan carried the Beretta in shoulder leather.

He had barely taken a dozen steps when a guy in a pristine tuxedo barred his way, blocking off one of the office doors. The face was expressionless, showing a deep tan that made the guy's pale eyes stand out. Bolan noted the spread of the shoulders as the hardman flexed his muscles.

"You don't come into this part of the casino. Just turn around and leave before I break an arm."

"That's not going to happen," Bolan said.

"You got a nerve coming in here."

Tuxedo slid his hand inside his jacket.

Bolan's response was instantaneous. His right fist lashed out and struck hard, crushing the guy's nose in an instant. Tuxedo gave a hoarse gasp as blood flowed down his face, tears welling in his eyes from the pain. His immobility gave Bolan his opening, and he struck a second time, catching the guy in his throat, reducing him to wheezing helplessness. Barely taking time for a breath, Bolan grabbed a handful of the guy's hair and yanked his head down into his rising knee. Tuxedo caught the powerful blow full-face. It snapped his head back and he went down without another sound.

Bolan stepped up to the door Tuxedo had been guarding. He could hear the murmur of voices inside.

The Executioner had no patience for protocol right now. He dismissed any notions of hurting anyone's feelings. This was not the time for following the rules of etiquette. He wanted to locate Marco Conte and went about it in the most direct way possible.

The office door was kicked clean off its hinges as Bolan burst through following a powerhouse boot from his foot. The splintered panel flew yards into the room, crashing into a nearby display cabinet and sending broken glass in all directions.

"Hey! What the fuck is—" one of the occupants said,

coming up off his seat, grabbing for the SIG-Sauer pistol he carried in a shoulder rig.

Bolan reached him before the weapon cleared the leather, the Beretta 93-R in his hand sweeping around in a brutal arc. The crunch as it connected with the *Mafiya* soldier's face could be heard across the room. The savage blow splintered the guy's jaw, sending a spray of blood and shattered teeth across the carpet. As the guy dropped, Bolan placed a 9 mm whispering slug in the back of his skull.

There were three other men in the room. Just seconds before they had been relaxing, enjoying Conte's whiskey and vodka. The sight of their buddy going down galvanized them into action.

The closest man to Bolan went for his hardware. The Beretta chugged and the hardman went down with a Parabellum slug in his thigh, bone shattered and flesh torn. As he struck the floor, he clawed at his hip for the weapon he carried. He barely touched the butt before Bolan's next shot spread pieces of his skull across the carpet.

The gunman next to him, hampered by a glass in one hand and a cigar in the other, dropped both items and made his own play. It lasted only as long it took Bolan to put him down with a slug to his chest. The guy toppled over backward, tangling with the chair he'd been using, and crashed to the floor.

The surviving hardman saw sense and held his hands away from his body, sweat suddenly beading his face as he stared into the Executioner's hard blue eyes.

"What the hell do you want?"

"Simple enough," Bolan said. "I want to know where Conte is. And you're going to tell me."

The guy managed a thin smile.

"If I do that, I'm as good as dead."

The Beretta moved.

"I can do that for you."

The tone of the voice said it all. The guy was in no mood for making jokes. What had already gone down confirmed that.

Bolan quickly frisked his captive, threw the handgun he found across the room, checked his ID and then stepped back again.

"You want to make a deal for your life, Kirov?"

"Okay, so I give Conte up. What next? You figure you can take him down? That's crazy. He has a bunch of guys to protect him. He's with Serge Bulova, and nobody moves against *him*. The man knows too many people."

"It's time for a change then." Bolan moved closer, the Beretta settling on its new target. "Your move, Karl."

Kirov stared into the muzzle of the Beretta. He understood how close he was to death and the thought obviously didn't sit well. Loyalty was a nice concept, and up until this moment Kirov had imagined as long as he was involved with Conte and the Bulova organization he was protected. That protection didn't seem so good with the barrel of a 9 mm Beretta up close and personal. All of Conte's influence and money didn't mean a damn thing. All it needed was for this man to pull the trigger and everything Kirov held dear went up in a blinding flash of pain.

"It comes down to a simple equation," Bolan said. "You add up what Conte and Bulova *might* have been able to offer against what I have right now. It doesn't take much working out. But at the end of the day you have to make your own choice."

"With that thing stuck in my face, Cooper?" he drawled, having finally figured out who Bolan was.

Kirov took a sideways glance at his former buddies. All down. All dead. No help there. His bosses were miles away protecting their own asses. He was caught in the middle. Self-preservation geared up and he knew his options were extremely limited.

"They're down in Florida," he said. "Bulova's backup place."

"Tell me exactly where."

Kirov laid it out for Bolan: the location, the number of shooters he had with him.

"He must have concerns if he's taken to hiding in the boonies."

"No kidding," Kirov said. "You have them both running scared. Conte wouldn't ever admit it, but taking off for Florida is a last resort."

"You can call your boss after I leave," Bolan said. "Make a wrong move, Karl, and you'll be out of the picture for good."

He wasn't concerned about the enemy being warned. It would let the mob higher-ups know that time was running out.

Bolan turned and left the office, exiting the way he'd entered. He holstered the 93-R as he headed for the door to the street. Nothing had changed in the casino. The constant, heavy noise had drowned any sound that might have leaked from the rear area.

Bolan walked out of the air-conditioned casino and paused on the sidewalk. He took out his sat phone and called Grimaldi.

"Hey, Sarge, what's the plan for today?"

"How are you fixed for a flight to Florida? I hear the climate can be pleasant this time of year. I have a location for Conte and Serge Bulova. It's a chance to clean out the rat's nest."

"The sunshine state? How soon do we leave?"

"Soon as possible, Jack. Just one thing. By the time we get there, they'll know we're on our way."

"Then we wouldn't want to disappoint them," Grimaldi said.

"That's what I was thinking."

"I'll be ready."

KIROV WAITED A quarter of an hour before he made the call. It was answered by one of Bulova's crew.

"I need to speak with Mr. Conte," Kirov said. *"Now."*

Kirov heard voices in the background before Marco Conte took the call.

"What is it?"

"He was at the casino. Cooper," Kirov said. "I was the only one who didn't get iced. The others are dead."

"And?"

"He's coming after you and Bulova."

Conte was silent for a moment.

"Does he know where I am?"

"Yeah," Kirov replied.

"You told him?"

"If I hadn't, he would have killed me, as well, Mr. Conte. I'm not ready to die even for you. Not like that. Money or no."

"A sensible answer," Conte said. "I admire a man with courage. Even if it is misplaced. It will not go unpaid."

The phone went dead in Kirov's hand. He sat for a while, unsure what lay ahead. The only thing he could be sure of—his fate couldn't be any worse than what lay ahead for Conte and Serge Bulova.

MARCO CONTE HELD the silent phone in his hand, aware it was trembling.

"Son of a bitch," he said. "Who the fuck does he think he is?"

"Who?"

Bulova had come into the room and was standing behind Conte.

"That guy. Cooper. He paid a visit to the casino and took out the crew I left waiting. That was Kirov on the phone. Cooper left him alive so he could deliver a message."

"He coming for us?"

"Yeah. Kirov gave us up to save his own miserable skin."

"He's not as dumb as he looks," Bulova said. "I must remember to tell him that when I have his throat ripped out."

"Serge, what do we do?"

Bulova laughed out loud. "Do? We make sure that guy receives a Florida welcome," he said. "Jesus, Marco, don't go all soft on me. I don't want you to forget it's because of your fucked-up handling of this mess that we're here. This Cooper asshole is coming all the way down here to play hero. Let's not disappoint him."

Bulova called for Danichev. When the man appeared, the mob leader informed him what was about to happen.

"That makes it easier for us," Danichev said. "I'll have the guys make ready to receive visitors. The way things have been happening they'll be pleased to get a chance at this bastard. They want major payback on the Feds for Killian and the others being taken out."

"No screwing around, Vitaly," Bulova instructed. "This Cooper is no weekend warrior. The guy knows his stuff, so don't get careless. I want him dead so we can feed him to the fishes."

"Don't worry, sir, we'll be waiting for him."

"Go set things up."

Conte was at the main window, staring out across the grounds. He knew the house and the area was well protected by the combined strength of his and Bulova's crews. They were well armed and there were enough of them to take on and defeat Cooper. Despite all that, he was still nervous. The guy seemed to have a knack for walking into danger and coming out the other side unscathed. Conte had to keep reminding himself that Cooper was still only one man.

One against many this time.

Those odds had to count for something, Conte told himself. So why wasn't he fully convinced?

They landed at a small Florida airstrip run by one of Jack Grimaldi's legion of flying acquaintances. Bernie Schindler was tall, lean and as tanned as cured leather. He greeted Grimaldi as if he was a long-lost brother, and when Bolan was introduced, Schindler shook his hand enthusiastically.

"A friend of Jack's is more than welcome," he said. "You got time for coffee?"

"After a flight with flyboy, here, I need something to calm my nerves," Bolan said.

"Still that bad, huh?"

Grimaldi was grinning as he stood behind Schindler. "Thanks for the vote of confidence, Cooper."

"Always a pleasure," Bolan said.

They trooped into the wooden shack that served as Schindler's charter office. He ran a couple of single prop aircraft as well as a Bell helicopter. From what Grimaldi had told Bolan, the guy made a reasonable living from his business, which sometimes ran close to the edge. Schindler ran the place with the help of a mechanic.

"Here you go, guys," Schindler said, handing over mugs of steaming black coffee. "The best you'll find in the state."

"Hate to drink and run, Bernie," Grimaldi said. "We're on a tight schedule today."

"No sweat, brother. I've got the wheels waiting around back. Now, she isn't the latest model but she's running hot and she'll get you where you need to go." Schindler handed over the key. "All gassed up and ready to roll."

Bolan took the key. "I'll go and load up," he said. "Thanks for the coffee, Bernie."

Leaving Grimaldi to keep Schindler talking, Bolan located the 4x4 and drove around to park beside the helicopter. He hefted two big gear bags and dropped them on the rear seat of the well-used vehicle. By the time he had the load settled, Grimaldi and Schindler were walking his way.

"Take it easy, guys," Schindler stated.

"See you later, bro," Grimaldi said as he took his place behind the wheel.

Schindler nodded. "Your chopper will be juiced up and ready to go when you get back." He sauntered away with a lazy wave.

Grimaldi drove the SUV out of the field and onto the road.

"Which way, boss?"

Bolan had his sat phone out, connecting to Stony Man where his signal was picked up, showing their position. Kurtzman, having already locked them onto the built-in satellite navigation system, had their route displayed.

"Follow the bouncing ball," Bolan said, showing Grimaldi the phone.

"On our way."

Their route took them around the outskirts of Miami, the city profile standing out against the late-afternoon sky. Grimaldi drove steadily, observing speed limits and making no maneuvers that might attract the attention of law enforcement.

This wasn't the first time Bolan had visited the area. Other missions had brought him to Florida on a number of occasions. He had encountered local cops previously and had come away with friendships intact. But he understood his position in relation to the on-site LEOs. If he could avoid any contact, he would do so, because where the *Mafiya* was concerned there might be cops on the payroll. As much as Bolan admired professional police officers, he was also well aware that there could be individuals on the take.

Cops taking bribes was far from being a fanciful myth. For whatever reasons, sometimes beyond their control, some lawmen decided to take the crooked track. Bolan's self-imposed refusal to ever strike out against peace officers was often sorely tried when he came up against the less-than-honest variety. He refused to drop the hammer on cops. Plain and simple, it was a point of honor as far as the Executioner was concerned. He had enough to handle with the real bad guys, so going for rogue cops was placed in a no-go zone.

Their line of travel took them through well-appointed residential areas: expensive homes that were built along the shore, gated communities where money bought lush lifestyles and reclusive anonymity.

"What do you reckon, Sarge? You fancy one of these places for your retirement?"

Bolan smiled at the suggestion.

Retirement didn't figure very often in his thoughts. He wasn't in some nine-to-five job where he clocked off each evening and drove home. Home and family seemed as far out reach as it ever had. Mack Bolan seldom considered those things. His life was what he was doing right now: traveling to yet another encounter with the Animal Man, the violators, the killers, the criminals who saw no problem when it came to indulging in wanton acts. They took what they wanted with little regard to the suffering they caused. Civilized existence with the rest of society was not on their agenda. It was Bolan's battles with evil that dictated the way his own life ran; a stable, ordered life was not part of the plan.

He surveyed the lines of houses, the gleaming vehicles parked in the driveways. He had no particular desire for any of those things.

He was content with his lot in life. Not for the first time Bolan understood the constraints his missions put on him. No matter how many times he faced death, no matter the way things came out, he would always be faced with yet another dire situation. There was no way he was going to bring an end to global or even homefront threats. He was one man who had taken up arms to confront evil in its many forms. The Executioner would take on each battle as it came, hoping that he made life just a little better with the defeat of each enemy.

"Not for me, Jack. Too quiet a life."

Grimaldi chuckled. He understood Bolan only too well. Not for him a sedentary life.

A few miles on, the moneyed homes slipped behind them. The road curved around the coastline. Vegetation grew thicker now, trees and foliage pushing in against the man-made strip of asphalt.

Bolan checked the phone display.

"Close, Jack," he said. "We need to go EVA while we have distance between us and Bulova's place. Find somewhere to park off the road. We can camouflage the vehicle and go in on foot."

Grimaldi chose a spot and eased off the road, taking the SUV into the shadowed confines of lush growth. When he turned off the engine, they picked up the soft rush of the surf brushing up to the nearby beach.

Out of the car Bolan opened a rear door and unzipped the gear bags. He stripped off his outer clothing to expose the blacksuit he was already wearing. He took off his shoes and replaced them with lace-up combat boots. Bolan donned a web harness and clipped on an assortment of ancillary weaponry that included a coiled garrote with hardwood grips, flash-bang grenades, military-spec grenades and thermite canisters. The razor-edged Tanto combat knife was housed in the sheath on his belt. He pocketed a few plastic riot cuffs and a compact transceiver that matched the one Grimaldi took.

His massive .44 Magnum Desert Eagle was holstered on his hip while the Beretta 93-R hung in shoulder leather. Bolan's rapid-fire weapon, which hung by its sling, was the Israeli-made 9 mm Uzi. With his weapons in place, checked and loaded, Bolan reached into the bag for extra magazines for his weapons, which he secured in pouches on his web harness.

Grimaldi, already clad in light tan combat pants and shirt, outfitted himself with ordnance. He had his Beretta 92-FS pistol and a similar model Uzi. The Stony Man pilot also carried a sheathed combat knife on his belt. He completed his change by pulling on a black ball cap that he snugged down comfortably.

They checked to ensure the transceivers were working, making sure the receiver-transmit settings were identical.

Bolan checked the light.

"We should have twilight in about an hour," he said. "That should allow us to move in close and get into position. If we come across any roving sentries, we need to take them down once we have full dark."

Grimaldi nodded.

"Smooth and quiet is the order of the day."

THEY MOVED AWAY from the SUV, swallowed by the overgrowth of trees and lush foliage. Underfoot the ground was soft and allowed them to move with barely a sound. Bolan took the lead with Grimaldi watching their back trail. Neither man spoke, aware of how well sound travels in silent terrain. They had worked together on many similar missions so there was little need for conversation.

They closed in on their target, and forty minutes in they were able to crouch in cover and observe Serge Bulova's Florida retreat.

The sprawling house was set well back from the road behind a four-foot wall that ran around three sides. The fourth side looked out across the shoreline, with a wide strip of empty beach and a jetty that reached beyond the breakwater. A thirty-foot boat was moored at the timber jetty. The house itself, on two levels, was constructed of timber and stone. A triple-car garage was attached to one side of the main structure.

Bolan and Grimaldi, concealed in the early evening, were able to spot the armed sentries moving around the house. They made a count of two covering the front, each carrying squat subguns and wearing shoulder rigs holding pistols.

"I think our mob honchos are feeling a little unappreciated right now," Grimaldi said.

"It's tough being at the top."

"So maybe we need to relieve them of some of that responsibility. This is your party, Sarge. Do you want to take the front entrance and let me go around back?"

Bolan nodded. He watched Grimaldi slip away into the fading light then concentrated his attention on the sentries roving the front of the property.

He studied their movements for long minutes, checking to see if the guards had any kind of regular pattern. It didn't take him long to establish that there was no pattern at all. He could understand why. The sentries were mob soldiers with no idea about strictly policing their areas. They were simply men with guns, most likely town, or city, inhabitants. Out here in the sticks, they stood out as having little cohesive experience for what they were doing.

Bolan eased his Uzi across his back. He slid the Tanto combat knife from its sheath and crept toward the house. He had noticed lights coming on in some of the rooms and paused when he reached the edge of the shrubbery. Ahead of him now was the open area fronting the house. He counted four parked SUVs in front of the building. They were top-of-the-range models, big, powerful vehicles that expressed the ostentatious lifestyles of their owners. Bolan decided the vehicles wouldn't be needed after his visit was over.

Bolan saw one of the guards moving his way. The guy was dressed in a gaudy floral shirt and pale slacks, lightweight loafers on his feet. Though he was covering his area, the expression on the sentry's face indicated he was less than enamored with the duty. His subgun hung loosely from one hand. The guy had an enormous cigar clenched between his teeth from which he blew thick clouds of smoke into the air.

Bolan checked on the guard closest to him, then saw the distant man turn and move out of sight behind the parked SUVs. Bolan's sentry came to within a couple of feet of the greenery shielding the Executioner. It was the best opportunity Bolan was going to get. He waited as the guy stopped, peered into the greenery, then turned to make his way back the way he had come. Bolan rose and stepped forward, reaching out with his left hand, the Tanto in his right.

The sentry, whether by instinct or dumb luck, suddenly came to a stop, tensing. He started to turn. Bolan struck, easing his hand around the guy's head and clamping it over his mouth, knocking the cigar clear. In the same instant of motion Bolan thrust the blade of his combat knife into yielding flesh, searching for and finding the jugular. One quick slash and it was over. He held the guard upright until his life drained away. Then he eased the man to the ground.

Sheathing the knife, Bolan grabbed the dead man's collar and slid him into the cover of the undergrowth. He picked up the dropped subgun and tossed it out of sight.

## 22

Jack Grimaldi edged along the side of the house to where it opened onto the back lawn and swimming pool. Sunlight danced across the smooth water in the blue-tiled pool.

Two men were in sight, dressed in casual clothing, sporting dark glasses and wearing holstered handguns. They stood at the edge of the pool in some kind of discussion.

Grimaldi keyed his transceiver and gave Bolan an update.

"I'm set to put these guys down, Sarge. Just give me the word."

"The word is go," Bolan said in response. "One is out of the picture here."

Grimaldi took his suppressor from a pocket and screwed it on to the threaded end of the Beretta's barrel. He pressed against the wall of the house and sighted down on the closer man, the 92-FS spitting out a single 9 mm slug. It impacted against the side of the target's skull, raising a mist of blood as it cored in and dropped the guy in a heap on the tiled edge of the pool.

The guy's partner was taken by surprise, his reaction slow, staring as his buddy went down, which allowed Grimaldi to resight and fire a second round from his pistol. The 9 mm bullet caught the man directly between the eyes, the impact kicking his head back. He slowly sank into a sitting position, then toppled backward and slid into the pool. The disturbed water rippled and a trail of diluted blood showed against the blue.

"Two down here," Grimaldi said into the transceiver.

BOLAN CLICKED OFF the transceiver after Grimaldi's report. He had picked up on the second guard moving out from the parked SUVs. Something in the way the guy was checking the area warned Bolan that he knew his partner was missing. He lifted his left hand and Bolan realized he was talking into a transceiver. After a brief conversation, the guard raised his subgun and headed in the general direction his now dead buddy had taken.

Time was running out fast.

Bolan went into action, knowing he had to take the initiative before the guard spotted him. He stepped out of cover, raised the Beretta and put a 3-round burst into the advancing sentry. They hit his chest and the man went down without resistance.

"Jack, I think we've been made," Bolan said into his transceiver.

"Copy that."

Bolan heard the squeal of tires on pavement. He turned to see the dark shape of a large sedan barreling in through the open gateway to the grounds. He had missed that; a vehicle posted on the road outside

the property, ready to respond to any problems within
or adjacent to the enclave. The heavy car rocked as it
swept in between the gate posts. Bolan made out two
people in the front.

The big sedan bounced as it hit a dip, sparks showing as it bottomed out. The vehicle powered across the
driveway and the sudden increase in speed caught Bolan
off guard. He had no chance to acquire a target. In the
last seconds he twisted his body to the side, the Buick
looming large. His move was barely enough to take him
out of the path of the speeding vehicle. It roared past,
clipping him, and Bolan felt himself rolling along the
ground before the impact bounced him in the air. He
spun, turned and threw out his free hand to brace his
fall. Using his agility, he pulled himself into a shoulder roll, gasping at the impact, and tumbled across the
uneven ground. He picked up the stench of rubber as
the car came to a screeching stop.

He knew he had only a short window of time before the occupants of the vehicle came for him. Bolan
still had the 93-R in his hand and he pushed it forward,
searching for movement. He saw the driver's door swing
open and a man exit the interior. The shooter clutched
a subgun in his left hand, his right sliding around to
catch the trigger.

Bolan upped the Beretta's muzzle, holding the pistol steady as he caught the man in his sights. He ignored the threat of the subgun and held his target for
the millisecond that gave him the advantage. The pistol
bucked in Bolan's hand as he stroked the trigger and
delivered three 9 mm slugs that hammered the target's
chest, pushing him back against the open door. The

*Mafiya* soldier slid across the door and dropped face-down on the driveway.

The passenger had ejected himself from his own seat, moving the length of the car and leaning across the trunk as his partner went down. He fired a fraction too fast and his burst pounded the ground inches away from Bolan's prone figure, sending chips of asphalt into the air.

The Executioner had pulled his 93-R around to pick up on the shooter, and he fired a burst that tore into his opponent's left shoulder, puncturing flesh and muscle. The hood jerked upright, his face twisting in pure shock. The Executioner adjusted his aim and fired another 3-round burst, this one delivered to the guy's throat and lower jaw. The hardman jerked back his head as blood jetted from severed arteries and fell out of sight behind the sedan.

Bolan pushed slowly to his feet, the Beretta leading the way as he closed in on the car. He checked out the driver first.

The Executioner kicked away the fallen weapon. The man's sightless eyes stared up at him as he double-checked for any sign of life. No movement.

Walking around the car, Bolan came up on the passenger from the rear, the 93-R covering the guy every step of the way. Bolan was moving slowly now, feeling the aches in his body following his headlong dive to the ground after the car had sideswiped him. His left shoulder pulsed with pain and there was a bleeding graze on his palm.

He stood over the second shooter, kicking his subgun aside. A wide pool of blood had crept out from around the guy's head, and started soaking into the ground. It had stopped flowing now, since his heart had shut down. The 9 mm slugs had made a mess of flesh and bone in the guy's neck and jaw.

"Two more who won't be collecting a pension, Bulova," Bolan said softly.

He holstered the Beretta and picked up one of the discarded P-90 subguns. An additional piece of hardware could come in handy in his present situation. Bulova appeared to have a plentiful supply of foot soldiers to sacrifice. As with most of his type, the Russian stayed away from the front line, simply sending out his minions to face danger—and in this case, death. It had always been that way. The top men gave the orders from their protected fortresses and allowed the less fortunate take the punishment. Nothing seemed to change.

Don't get too comfortable, Bulova, Bolan thought. Your turn is coming. He clicked his transceiver. "I'm going in the front, Jack," he said.

BOLAN WAS IN Florida to take down Bulova and Conte once and for all.

This was no mission to secure information. The soldier already had what he needed. Conte and the Russian *Mafiya* overlord's time was running out. Bolan had already done a great deal of damage to the organization. This time around he was determined to end it. The criminal bosses would not be calling their lawyers to cover their asses. Legal chicanery was out the window. Bulova and Conte were not about to call the shots this time. They had showed disdain for civilized dealings, so he had brought down the thunder that only the one-man force known as the Executioner could deliver.

As Bolan crouched by the bulk of the parked SUVs,

facing Bulova's house, he felt the first drops of rain brought by the rising wind sweeping in from the nearby Atlantic shore. The rainfall rolled off the waterproof blacksuit as it quickly built. The rain was nothing Bolan couldn't handle. It would add to his natural cover, making it uncomfortable for any of Bulova's people out tramping the grounds.

Without warning, powerful lights mounted at roof level burst into life, lighting up the front of the house and grounds.

Bolan saw an armed guard move out from the double front doors as he stepped into the glare of one of the spotlights. The guy had turned up the collar of his expensive suit against the light rain and held his subgun tight against his chest. His movements told Bolan he was unhappy with his current situation. That suited Bolan. Let the guy come.

The illumination provided by the security lights showed him the sweep of the open driveway.

The house windows were ablaze with light. Bulova was obviously determined to surround himself with illumination, removing any dark corners that an invader might use. Bolan wondered how many guns the man had inside the house. He didn't allow the lack of knowledge to faze him.

Once he made his move he would find out.

The guard who had exited the front door had paused just a few feet away to search the area. He had to have seen the bodies from the car but made no move to check them out. He simply spoke into the headset he wore, reporting to someone in the house.

Bolan waited with the patience he had acquired over years of experience. During his military service, he had learned the art of long surveillance. His time as a sniper had called for infinite patience. Watching and waiting for the right moment for a designated target to appear had called for the ability to settle and bring the mind and body into a calm state, to regulate breathing and cultivate the ability to view everything with clarity. Those attributes were still with Bolan. They had not faded with time.

The Executioner unzipped a pocket and withdrew a matte-black suppressor, threading it onto the Beretta's muzzle. He set the pistol for single shot then waited.

The guard was three steps away from the door. Over the man's shoulder Bolan could see that a second guard had stepped outside to stand behind his partner.

The Executioner raised the 93-R, extending his arm, and centered the muzzle on his first target. His finger stroked the trigger. The Beretta uttered a discreet cough and a neat, round hole appeared between the eyes of the first guard. He took half a step before his motor functions shut down and he toppled forward. The second man brought up his weapon, his eyes searching. He took a silenced 9 mm slug to the forehead and fell back against the wall.

Bolan edged around the SUVs and cut across to the partly open doors.

GRIMALDI HAD BEEN halfway to the patio doors when the powerful spotlights came on. Midway across the stone slabs, he'd seen no point in retreat.

He crossed the patio in long strides. He had seen movement on the other side of the glass doors and was aware the enemy could spot him at any moment.

The Stony Man pilot wanted to be in a better position before the man behind the door came closer. The Beretta was in both hands, tracking in on the target. Grimaldi was well in range when the man moved forward and he wasn't about to offer the guy any leeway. This was a do or die mission for him and Bolan. Taking the offensive was the best—the only—option.

The black muzzle of the 92-FS zeroed in. Grimaldi triggered his shot and saw the guy's head jerk to one side as the Parabellum round cored in through flesh and bone to ravage the brain. The guy dropped without a murmur, his arms splayed wide.

Grimaldi was committed now. There was no backing off.

Just before Bolan stepped in through the front doors he crouched and picked up one of the discarded FN P-90 subguns from the closer man he had put down. He released the 5.7 mm, 50-round magazine and tucked it behind his belt. It gave him the additional firepower he might need once he breached the house—his next objective.

The hand-carved double front doors swung open under Bolan's push. As the high doors flew back, the Executioner tossed in one of his flash-bang grenades, pulling back to the wall outside and briefly covering his ears. The grenade had bounced along the wide entrance hall, so he was out of range as the harsh crack echoed and brilliant light filled the space. The second the noise abated Bolan went inside, the P-90 probing ahead.

One hardman was slumped against the wall, his eyes streaming from the effects of the flash-bang. He stared unseeing at Bolan as the Executioner appeared and fumbled with the subgun in his hands. Bolan put him down with a short burst from the P-90, the guy skittering along the wall, leaving bloody streaks from exit wounds.

Halfway along the hall, a wide staircase led to the next floor. Two gunners came into view at the top of the flight, weapons coming on line. Autofire crackled, slugs chewing at the polished floor and kicking up splinters of wood. But by the time the shooters reacted to his presence, Bolan had moved, flattening against the far wall, his P-90 angled up to deliver a concentrated burst that shredded the banister and ripped into yielding flesh. The pair of shooters was pushed back, blood coursing from their open wounds.

A third hardman stood on the landing, emerging from the side passage, and Bolan caught him before the guy could pull back, raising the subgun and firing. The burst caught the guy in the side of his head, tearing out flesh and bone that erupted from his skull in a bloody gush. The guy fell to his knees then collapsed in an untidy heap.

A visual inspection showed Bolan that he still had fifty percent of ammunition in the magazine. He checked a door on his right then kicked it open. Empty. Bolan moved on after tossing in a prepped thermite canister. He heard the dull sound of the canister igniting, starting to spew its white-hot load.

To his left, on the opposite side of the hallway, a door was slowly cracked open a few inches, the black muzzle of a weapon sliding into view. Bolan brought his P-90 around and punched a burst through the door panel. He heard a pained grunt as his slugs found a target on the other side of the door. Bolan executed a rapid magazine change before he booted the door open and launched a fragmentation grenade inside the room. The gren detonated with a hard crack as he moved away from the door, his weapon probing ahead of him, searching for more targets.

A set of double doors stood directly ahead. Bolan picked up frantic voices. Someone was shouting orders in Russian.

He hit the center of the doors with his shoulder, momentum carrying him into a large room as the heavy doors swung wide.

Bolan had a swift glimpse of book-lined shelves, expensive furniture, a generous wet bar with a curving wood counter and stacked shelves behind it. To his left stood a large, hand-carved wooden desk and a scattering of leather armchairs.

Behind the desk, sitting in a hand-tooled leather chair, was Serge Bulova, clad in a well-tailored suit, silk shirt and sober silk tie. Seated beside the desk, his face fish-belly white, was Marco Conte. Bolan recognized Milo Forte, Conte's bodyguard, standing beside his boss. Fronting the crime boss were his personal minions, all well dressed, hard-faced and wielding drawn weapons.

They had all turned in the direction of the doors the moment they had burst open.

Four hardmen were ready to earn their pay.

But all of them were too slow when it came to face the black-clad Executioner.

Bolan's P-90 made a wide sweep, the muzzle spitting fire as he unleashed a relentless burst of 5.7 mm death. The 50-round magazine expended itself on the quartet, hammering the deadly slugs into their flesh, splitting bone and pulverizing internal organs.

In the seconds it took to put the four hardmen down, not one of them managed to get off a single shot. Bolan's action had been too fast to counter. Bloody and gasping from shock, the members of Bulova's protection squad were left sprawling across the expensive carpet, spilling their blood in a final—impotent—gesture.

As the last man fell, Bolan tossed aside the empty P-90 and swung the 9 mm Uzi from where it hung at his back, his finger curling around the trigger as he leveled the weapon at Bulova, Conte and Forte. In the same movement, Bolan stepped to one side of the open doors and pressed himself against the wall in a protective move.

Bulova glanced down at the tear in his coat sleeve where one of Bolan's slugs had clipped it. When he looked up, the Executioner could see the sweat showing on his fleshy face.

"You know how much this suit cost?" the Russian asked.

"Too much for someone like you, Bulova."

The mob boss pushed to his feet, thrusting a finger at Bolan.

"No one speaks to me like that... You come into my house. You kill and destroy."

"I set fire to it, as well."

Bolan plucked a second thermite grenade from his harness. He pulled the safety then tossed the canister out of the door where it rolled across the hall floor.

"After today you won't be needing the house," he said. "Just as a point of interest, we located the files Harry Sherman got from Conte's computer. The Justice Department can't believe their luck. All that evidence. Your business is done, Bulova, so, though it's the end of you, you can take solace in knowing that all of your crooked friends will be paying for their association with you."

Bulova's eyes widened in alarm as the grenade burst and began spewing the deadly thermite compound.

"My lawyers will see you in jail for this."

"Unless your lawyers have buckets and plenty of water to douse the fires, Bulova, there isn't a damn thing they can do for you."

"Then we should talk," Bulova said, maintaining an even tone. "You have to realize how powerful I am. What I can offer you. This place is nothing. Just a house I use when I need to get away from the daily grind."

"And there I was thinking it was a bolt-hole for a couple of runaways."

"I like a man with a sense of humor. And you interest me, Cooper. I want to know who you are."

"Just a house cleaner come to take out the garbage. I like a tidy ending. And cremation does that."

Marco Conte pushed to his feet. His panic was obvious. Any semblance of control he might have had was gone.

"You don't want me," he said. "I just run a casino in Vegas."

Bolan glanced at him, the muzzle of the Uzi moving to cover the man.

"Gambling? I see you've forgotten about the drugs. The prostitution. Slave trade. All the other rackets you front, Conte."

"You don't understand, Cooper. I don't have a choice. It's Bulova. He sets the deals. He's—"

Serge Bulova lashed out with his right hand, catching Conte full in the face. The force of the blow sent the casino boss stumbling back, falling to his knees, blood coursing down his face where the heavy gold rings Bulova wore had ripped his flesh.

Forte, deciding he was failing his employer, stepped forward to help Conte stand. As he bent, he snaked out the pistol concealed under his suit coat. He wasn't fast enough. Bolan hit him with a short burst and put the big man down.

Bulova raged at the dazed Conte. "You worthless piece of shit. I should have had you put down years ago. Even now all you can do is try to save your own fucking skin."

The *Mafiya* head man lunged for one of the desk drawers, yanking it open and snatching up a SIG-Sauer P-226 pistol. He worked the slide, lifting the weapon, his expression wild and triumphant. He angled the weapon down at Conte and pulled the trigger, driving a pair of slugs into Conte's skull.

The Uzi barely moved. Bolan touched the trigger and loosed a burst that hit the hand holding the pistol. Bulova's hand transformed into a bloody mess. The mobster howled in anguish, clutching his crippled hand to his chest, covering it with his left hand. He ignored the blood staining his expensive suit as he slumped back in his executive chair.

The old Bulova emerged from the pain as he faced Bolan.

"You will regret this…"

"No. It's over. Today is judgment day and the jury's out. And you, Serge Bulova, have been found guilty."

Bulova uttered a ragged laugh. "You talk like a judge. Who are you to speak of guilt to me?" His eyes blazed with defiance. "You are nothing…" Without another word the mob boss lunged out of his chair.

Bolan fired a short burst directly at Bulova's face. The force of the bullets took off the top of his head. The mobster's body arched in protest just before it sank to the floor.

"Wrong," Bolan said. "I'm your executioner."

He reloaded the Uzi.

Behind him the hall was a rising maw of hungry fire as the thermite canister spit out its unquenchable contents. The carpeted stairway was alight. The room Bolan had firebombed earlier was fully involved now, the flames licking at walls and ceiling.

The Executioner crossed the room. He let the Uzi dangle from its sling and picked up one of the chairs. He launched it at the picture window, smashing the glass from the frame. He was able to step over the low sill and out onto the driveway. He turned his Uzi on the parked SUVs, riddling the expensive bodywork and windows, reducing the tires to shredded rubber.

"Jack, do you copy?" Bolan said into his transceiver.

"I hear you, Sarge."

"You clear of the house?"

"Coming your way as we speak."

When Grimaldi appeared, he was leading a quartet of subdued young women. They were wide-eyed with shock as they clustered around Grimaldi.

"I found these young ladies at the rear of the house. In-house entertainment."

"As if we had any choice," one of the women said. "Those creeps dragged us here out of their club. It was do what they said or…"

"They won't bother you again," Bolan said.

"Hey, are you guys cops? Feds?"

"I don't care who you are," another woman said. "Please just get us away from here."

"We'll give you a ride back to town," Bolan stated. "Is that okay with you, ladies?"

"As long as we can get out of this rain, it's fine," the first woman said. "I thought Florida had sunshine all the time."

"Even Florida has its off days," Grimaldi commented.

"I heard guns. It was like a war zone." The woman's tone hardened. "Did you cap that asshole Bulova? I hope you did. Tell me you did. I can still feel his creepy hands on me."

"Ladies, Bulova and his crew won't be bothering anyone again," Grimaldi said.

There were no further confrontations with any of Bulova's crew. Bolan decided he and Grimaldi had either forced survivors to back away or the men they had faced down had been Bulova's entire local force.

They walked away from the house and back through the trees to where he and Grimaldi had parked their SUV. By the time they had reached the vehicle, a heavy pall of smoke and sheets of flame were rising above Serge Bulova's house.

"It burns well," one of the young women said as they crowded into the SUV. Bolan stood at the tailgate and stripped off his ordnance, pulled on his leather jacket and joined Grimaldi, taking the front passenger seat.

Once they were on the road, Bolan took out his sat phone. After a quick word with Price he asked to be connected with Brognola. The big Fed's weary voice came through.

"Busy day?" Bolan asked.

"Busy enough but most likely not as hectic as yours. Anything left standing in Florida?"

"That could hurt if I thought you meant it," Bolan said quietly so that the women wouldn't be able to make out his words. "We're done here. We took care of business."

"Bulova and Conte?"

"Yeah. There's going to be some jockeying for the thrones now. It's time to use that information on Sherman's flash drive. We need to make good use of it, Hal. I don't like to think he died for nothing."

"Leo already has a transcript of everything on those files, and Justice is working up a task force to go after a string of names. There will be some shocks when the arrests start."

"The lawyers are the ones who'll benefit once they're hired for the defense."

Brognola's laugh was short and tinged with some bitterness.

"That's the way of it, Striker. When these things start to roll, some people just lawyer up. Others step behind their positions and hope they can walk away. Leo almost died. Harry Sherman did. What the hell, Striker, it's a world of compromise in the end. We get to bring some bad guys down. We lose out with others. And we have to take the knocks because we're on the *good* side."

"Bulova and Conte aren't walking away from it this time," Bolan said.

"Thanks to you," Brognola said. "Can't say there'll be much in the way of tears about that."

"Jack and I are on our way home. Just a couple of things." Bolan explained about the young women. He also managed to mention the fact that Bulova's house was well on the way to being razed.

Brognola listened in silence then said, "Leave it with me. I'll see to it the local law is updated. I don't see any rush to have the fire department alerted. They can sift through the ashes when the place cools down. Justice can step in and deal with any fallout. I suggest you and Jack get out of Florida once you drop off the young ladies. You got anything else to clear up?"

"I need to see Gwen Darrow. Check on how she's doing. I can drop in on Marshal Carson while I'm there. And I'll have a word with Laura. They need to know Harry made good on his promise to hand over his evidence. Even posthumously."

"They'll appreciate that," Brognola said. "Be here when you get back."

# Epilogue

Harry Sherman had paid a heavy price with his defiance of Conte and Bulova's organization. But before his untimely death he had carried through with his promise to deliver. Gwen and her daughter needed to know that despite his being dragged into a mess with the mob, Harry had not lost sight of the end game.

Bolan stared out the rain-streaked windshield. He was feeling the weariness that flooded his veins after the unrelenting activities of the past few days. The removal of pressure did that to him. He made himself a promise to take some R&R once he wrapped up the mission. Just a little down time, a couple of days, so he could refresh his mind and body away from the hell grounds. Maybe some back-country skiing or hiking.

He relished his brief time away from what he saw, and accepted, as his chosen world. Any free time he had would be short. There was still work to be done. Always.

Mack Bolan would be ready to face it when it came his way.

\* \* \* \* \*

# UPCOMING TITLES FROM

## THE EXECUTIONER
### DON PENDLETON'S

**MISSILE INTERCEPT** – *Don Pendleton*
*Available June 2016*
Two American scientists are kidnapped just as North Korea
makes a play for Cold War–era ballistic missiles. Determined to
save the scientists and prevent a world war, Bolan learns he's
not the only one with his sights set on retrieving the missiles…

**TERRORIST DISPATCH** – *Don Pendleton*
*Available September 2016*
Atrocities continue in the Ukraine and the adjoining
Crimean Peninsula, annexed by Russia in March 2014. With no
end in sight, a plan is hatched to force American involvement
by sending Ukrainian militants to strike Washington, DC, killing
civilians and seizing the Lincoln Memorial as protest against
their homeland's threat from Russia. Can Bolan bring the war
home to the plotters' doorstep?

**COMBAT MACHINES** – *Don Pendleton*
*Available December 2016*
What began in a Romanian orphanage twenty years earlier,
when a man walked away with ten children and disappeared,
leads Mack Bolan and a team of Interpol agents to fend off a
group of "invisible" assassins carving their way across Europe…
toward the USA.

Another cartel guard leaned around the corner of one of
the trucks and brought up his weapon. But before he could
fire, the Executioner sent a zipping stitch of rounds across
the man's chest. He tumbled forward. Across the room,
Martinez and his team brought down two more hostiles.

An eerie silence descended over the room. Bolan,
Martinez and the rest of the marines continued to clear
the warehouse, encountering no apparent resistance.

Grimaldi's voice sounded in Bolan's ear mic. "There's
a firefight going on at the airstrip. Looks like that plane is
turning around for a takeoff."

Bolan glanced at Martinez. "There's trouble at the
airstrip."

"Go! We've got this one covered."

The Executioner nodded and worked his way outside,
moving with caution and deliberation as he inserted a
fresh magazine into his weapon. Ahead, he could see
flashes of gunfire. The twin propellers of the plane were
spinning with increasing power as the aircraft started to
move.

"Want me to do a flyover to try to keep them on the
ground?" Grimaldi asked.

"Go for it," Bolan said.

Grimaldi buzzed the airstrip, diving at the accelerating plane.

The aircraft jerked to the left, slowing. The side door flew open and a figure jumped to the ground. Thin streams of red tracer rounds zoomed upward.

"Whoever the hell that guy is," Grimaldi said over the radio, "I'm taking fire, and it's coming close!"

Bolan paused, acquired a sight picture of the hostile gunner and squeezed off a quick burst. The man twisted in Bolan's direction, and the Executioner fired again. His target jerked slightly. He was hit—but how badly?

Seconds later he had his answer as the red tracer rounds began zipping past him. He ducked, rolled to the left and came up on one knee just as the firing stopped. He saw the hostile leaning back, his right arm extended behind him.

Grenade! Bolan fired another burst, and seconds later the flash and concussion of an explosion washed over him, accompanied by a second larger conflagration as the plane went up in a gigantic fireball.

*Don't miss*
*MISSILE INTERCEPT by Don Pendleton,*
*available June 2016 wherever*
*Gold Eagle® books and ebooks are sold.*